"A Greek do[...]
forgive or forget."

Andreas spoke coldly, and his harsh features were frightening in their anger. "I have been planning this revenge for many years. What your father did to me was more unforgivable."

"I—I would like to lie down," Regan said dully. "I'm not feeling well." She put her hand to her aching temple.

"Poor Regan," he taunted. "What a shock for you. To come here thinking you are simply starting a new job when in fact you are to become my wife. A dutiful one, I hope."

"Never!" Her eyes flashed at him. "I don't intend being meek—in bed or out of it."

His green eyes suddenly sparked with undisguised interest. "I will like that," he said. "Yes. I will like that very much...."

CAROLE MORTIMER
is also the author of these

Harlequin Presents

CAROLE MORTIMER

devil lover

Harlequin Books

TORONTO • LONDON • LOS ANGELES • AMSTERDAM
SYDNEY • HAMBURG • PARIS • STOCKHOLM • ATHENS • TOKYO

Harlequin Presents edition published May 1981
ISBN 0-373-10430-8

Original hardcover edition published in 1981
by Mills & Boon Limited

CHAPTER ONE

ONCE AGAIN REGAN CHECKED the address written on the piece of paper in her hand, sure that the building in front of her couldn't possibly be the place. The girl at the agency must have made a mistake; this quiet building set in the exclusive part of London couldn't possibly be the right place for her interview to be taking place. And yet the address appeared to be right.

A man was sitting at a desk just inside the thickly carpeted reception area, probably there to keep out undesirables. The logical thing to do would be to see if she fitted into that category.

The old man listened politely while she made her query. "I'm not sure," she said nervously, "but I think a Mr. Western is expecting me for an interview this afternoon. Apartment four."

"And your name?"

"Miss Thomas," she supplied with a smile. At least he hadn't thrown her straight out. "Safe Employment sent me."

He smiled back at her, a man obviously of retirement age who probably found this job suited his advanced years. He wouldn't have too much to do; the building only consisted of four luxury apartments. Regan admired him for continuing employment when he no longer needed to—too many old people had no choice but to remain at home with the high number of unemployed, and usually gave up the will to live not long after. This man, although probably in his early seventies, gave the impression of a zest for life, a youthful twinkle in the faded blue eyes.

"Mr. Western is expecting you, Miss Thomas." He put her mind at rest about it being the right location. Thank God it was the right place; it was already five to three and the appointment was for three o'clock! "Would you like me to take you up," he offered, "or can you find your own way?"

"I'll find my own way." She thanked him, thinking of the wear on his legs . . . as he was probably doing.

She wasn't sure it was worth her attending the interview now that she had seen the wealthy background of her prospective employer. She felt sure he would require the very best qualifications from the person chosen to be the companion to his daughter. She would be in the nature of a governess really, but she didn't think a charge of nearly sixteen years of age would consider a girl of twenty old enough to fit that description. The girl probably considered herself old enough not to need a companion *or* governess. Not that Regan could blame her, but apparently the father was often away on business and didn't consider his elderly relatives capable of caring for his daughter. The mother was dead.

But now that Regan had seen the quiet opulence that surrounded her charge, she didn't think she stood a chance of being employed by the father. She had done a college course in child care, but had no actual experience of working with children other than the necessary fieldwork during the course. Mr. Western appeared to be wealthy enough to employ only the best for his daughter, and with no experience to back her up, Regan could hardly be called that.

The door to apartment four was opened by a maid in a smart black-and-white uniform, the simple white painted door in no way hinting at the elegance and wealth evident in every article in the huge room she was ushered into. Her feet sank into the thickly carpeted

floor of a particularly attractive honey shade, the deep
brown leather suite placed strategically around the
room, and the sofa large enough to seat at least five people. It was a beautiful room, beautifully furnished, with
the long coffee table a beautiful antique. But it was a
room that lacked something, lacked the vital something
she believed necessary to make it a home. But probably
Mr. Western was away so often he didn't have the time
to make it a home. Regan's heart went out to the
daughter of the house, her emotions already becoming
involved.

She sat gingerly on the edge of one of the sumptuous
armchairs while the maid disappeared into one of the
other rooms, probably an office or study, to tell Mr.
Western of her arrival. She looked down nervously at
the smart green suit and crisp white blouse she wore,
seeing a certain marmishness about her clothing, but
knowing they gave her a coolly assured appearance, for
all of her youth. She had no doubt her usual attire
would be frowned on, the tight jeans and pullovers that
emphasized every curve of her body.

"Miss Thomas?"

She stood up slowly, straightening her skirt as she did
so. The male voice was pitched low and attractive, and a
hasty glance at the newcomer showed him to be a tall
man in his early thirties, with short blond hair brushed
back off his brow, blue eyes twinkling in friendly
examination, and the mouth curved into an attractive
smile. Regan felt some of the tension leave her as she
returned his smile.

She accepted his proffered hand. "I'm Regan
Thomas, yes," she acknowledged huskily.

"Clive Western." He gave her hand a hearty shake.
"Please, sit down. I've asked Margaret to provide us
with some tea. I'm sure you could do with some," he
smiled understandingly.

"That will be lovely." At least the job didn't appear

to have already been taken by what she felt sure must be numerous applicants. Unless the tea was supposed to lessen the disappointment when she was told the position had been filled.

She looked up once again only to find Clive Western's admiring glance on her. She knew her auburn hair, that when loose waved down to her shoulder blades but at the moment was styled into a smooth bun at her nape, uptilted blue eyes surrounded by thick dark lashes, turned-up nose and wide smiling mouth, made up an attractive if not beautiful young woman when complemented by her slim, curvaceous figure, but she wasn't sure she welcomed her possible future employer noticing such things. But maybe he hadn't; maybe she was being oversensitive about this first interview. What did it matter if she didn't get the job; just this interview would be some experience to take on to her next one.

"The girl at the agency tells me this will be your first job." Clive Western sat down opposite her, crossing one well-clad foot over the other.

Her eyes brightened. So the job hadn't been taken. Maybe she could still get on a short list or something. "Yes," she answered shyly. "I only left college a couple of weeks ago."

He nodded. "So the agency explained. They also said you had no objections to moving out of London."

"None at all." She was beginning to feel a little more confident. "In fact, until a couple of years ago I lived in Norfolk...and that is definitely out of London," she added mischievously.

"Indeed," he nodded. "But I'm afraid it would be the other way—Cornwall, in fact."

"It wouldn't matter. The aunt and uncle I lived with moved up to Scotland a few months after I came here. One of my cousins got a job up there and as my uncle was retired the whole family decided to go."

"But not you?"

She was aware that she was being led, but she was also aware that this man had a right to know her background. After all, she might possibly become his daughter's constant companion. "I had already been accepted for a college course here."

"And you haven't considered joining them now?" He indicated she should pour the tea the maid had just brought in, which she did, leaving him to add his own sugar if he wanted it. He didn't.

"I didn't really see the point, not as my job usually involves living in."

"And time off?"

"Holidays I spend with them, but weekends I usually spend with the friends I've made here."

"And will you be leaving anyone special behind?"

"A boyfriend, you mean?" She watched him nod. "No one who really counts." She hoped Donny would forgive her for that. She wasn't seriously interested in him, although he didn't treat their friendship with the same casualness. He was one of the reasons she didn't mind leaving London. Mere words didn't seem to be enough to convince him of her disinterest in making things more serious between them.

"Good, good," he nodded again, studying the tip of one highly polished shoe. His ease didn't fool Regan for one minute; there was an astute brain behind his polite manner, a brain that missed little. "And what do you know of Helena?"

"The little girl?"

Clive Western smiled. "I don't somehow think she would like being called that."

"I'm sure she wouldn't," Regan laughed, her cheeks flushed in her embarrassment. "My professors wouldn't be very pleased with me if they had heard that slip-up. I meant to say young lady."

"I'm sure you did." His mouth quirked with humor. "And yes, Helena is the young lady. Although I

wouldn't really call her that, either," he added thoughtfully.

"I know very little of her, except her age and that her
mother is dead."

"Gina died just over ten years ago."

"I'm sorry," Regan said softly.

"It was rough on Helena," he agreed. "She was only
five when her mother walked out on her."

"Walked out . . .? I'm sorry, I thought you said—"

"Oh, I did. Please, help yourself." He indicated the
plate of delicious-looking pastries on the tea wagon.
"You don't look as if you have to watch what you eat."

"No, I don't. But I—I won't if you don't mind." She
always ended up with more cream over her than inside
her, and she didn't want to make a fool of herself when
the interview seemed to be going so well. "I've just
eaten lunch," she excused, the silent rumblings of her
tummy telling her that it had been over three hours ago.
And the pastries did look delicious!

Clive Western shrugged. "To get back to Gina." He
frowned. "She had already gone back to America,
alone, before the accident happened."

"I see."

"The marriage was—well, it wasn't a success. I'm
telling you this because you may find Helena won't take
kindly to a female being introduced into her world, not
a female she has to take notice of, anyway. She's been
surrounded by just men for so long now—staff, tutors,
her father—that I'm afraid she's rather an independent
young girl. She's attractive enough; she just needs a
push in the right direction to make her into a beautiful
young woman."

"She resents the idea of a companion," Regan said
with a sigh. This job was certainly turning out to have a
lot of the pitfalls that had been described to her during
her recent course.

"She resents any idea of change," Clive Western corrected. "But things can't go on as they have been. She's running wild down there in Cornwall. But the business is very time-consuming, requiring a lot of time traveling to our different branches all over the world. The personal appearance has never done any harm, and it certainly keeps the employees on their toes. They never know when the boss is going to walk in."

"And, er, what is the business?"

"Shipping, hotels, holidays."

Wow! No wonder he looked as if he were made of money. "So Helena spends a lot of her time on her own?"

He nodded. "Except for the staff down there."

"She's never had a companion before?"

"Years ago. Then she went to boarding school for a time. A bad bout of flu turning to pneumonia put a stop to that just over a year ago. Since then she's been tutored at home. She's supposed to be delicate," he added dryly.

Regan frowned. "But she has a tutor living down there with her?"

"Yes."

"Then I really don't see.... When would I get to do my job?" She looked and sounded puzzled.

"Helena only studies until three in the afternoon; after that her time is her own. Her tutor is a male, so that would be the time you took over."

"But I—what would I do all day until she had finished her schoolwork?"

"Walk, sunbathe, anything that you like doing."

She shook her head. "I really don't think you need someone like me. Isn't there a relative or friend who could go and stay with her until she's well enough to return to school, someone who could be a friend to her, share things with her? If I accepted this job I wouldn't be earning my money." She knew the salary already, and it was a very good one. All the more reason not to accept it under false pretenses.

"Oh, but you would," he assured her. "It would merely be a reversal of the day. Up until three o'clock your time would be your own, but after that, until Helena goes to bed about ten, you would be with her. Weekends you would be expected to be with her all day."

"I see." That changed things. The way he put it it sounded a reasonable arrangement. Just a reversal of the day, as he said.

"So, would you be willing to take the job?"

"Yes, I—I think so." It all seemed to be happening so fast. "But don't you have other applicants to see first?" What was she trying to do, see herself out of what looked like being a very interesting job?

"There are no other applicants. The job wasn't advertised, and the agency doesn't have anyone else to send. Now that I've told you all the drawbacks, are you still interested in the job?"

"Oh, yes." Her eyes glowed brightly blue.

"Good," he grinned. "Now I'll tell you some of the good things about it. The salary you already know. You would have more or less a free hand with Helena. The staff down there would treat you more or less as the mistress of the house, and once you've got over Helena's initial antagonism, I think you'll find she can be quite a loyal friend. Now what's your answer?"

"I think," she told him shyly, "that I would like the job."

"Then that's settled," he said with satisfaction and obvious relief. He held out the plate of sticky pastries she had earlier refused. "Have a cake to celebrate. I'd offer you something stronger, but then I'd have to join you, and as I still have a certain amount of work to do today.... Go on, have one," he encouraged as she still hesitated. "I'm going to have one," he added enticingly.

Regan laughingly took a chocolate eclair, her

favorite. "I bet you and Helena are great friends," she smiled. "You seem to have a way with females."

He shook his head. "I'm afraid Helena is off me at the moment."

"She's at an awkward age. I'm sure she'll soon get over whatever it is you've done to upset her."

"Not that little lady. Helena isn't one to forget anything, but then neither is her father."

Regan finished her pastry, wiping her chocolate covered fingers on the napkin. Ordinarily she would have licked them clean, but she couldn't do that in front of this man. It just wasn't fair how he managed to eat his without even seeming to get in the least sticky. And he didn't look in the least like a man who would bear a grudge. But then, what did she really know about him? Nothing, except the polite friendly side of his character he had shown during this interview.

"When could you start work?" he asked now.

She shrugged. "Whenever you want me to. I've been taking a holiday since college finished, but that's over now. I can start at any time."

"Let's see, today is Thursday. I have to drive down on Sunday to pick up a few things. Could you be ready to go by then?"

It would take a bit of organizing, but she would do it somehow. "That would be fine," she nodded.

"Nine o'clock suit you?"

Goodness, on a Sunday, too! "Anytime that suits you," she assured him. Her first interview and she had got the job! It was fantastic.

"Then nine o'clock it is. It's quite a drive, pretty hazardous toward the end. The house is quite remote, with very minor roads the last ten miles or so. I usually stay to lunch and leave straight after."

"That can't give you much time with Helena."

"Enough," he grimaced. "A little of Helena goes a

long way. Sorry,'' he grinned. "I mustn't put you off before you start.''

It wasn't putting her off at all. His aversion to spending time with his daughter reminded her of her own father's absences during her own childhood, and her sympathies all lay with Helena. Her father had been a busy man, too, traveling the world for his work and pleasure, and in the ten years of her life before he was killed she had probably seen him for a year of that time. Aunt Edith and Uncle Fred had brought her up as their own daughter, and although her father had often mocked them for their staidness, they had had no hesitation in adopting her when her father had died.

"I haven't put you off, have I?'' Clive Western must have noticed the shadows in her eyes.

"Not at all,'' she answered coolly. "I'm looking forward to meeting Helena.''

"That's fine, then.'' He stood up in conclusion of the interview. "I'm sorry to rush you, but I have another appointment at four o'clock.'' He gave her a warm smile.

Regan stood up, too, her handbag clutched primly in front of her. She still couldn't believe she had got this job! "Are you sure I'll be suitable?'' she asked anxiously. "My qualifications—''

"Already discussed with the agency. I'll let them know you've accepted the job.''

"I'm sure you're too busy—''

"They will want their fee, Miss Thomas,'' he interrupted dryly. "Which means I have to contact them, anyway.''

"Oh—oh, yes.'' She blushed at her stupidity.

"Sunday, then?''

"Yes,'' she confirmed.

She was still smiling when she walked past the man in the reception area, receiving a smile back. She called in and did some shopping before going back to the apartment she shared with Lindy. She was in the kitchen when she heard her friend's key in the lock an hour later.

Lindy burst into the room. "Did you get it?" She pulled out the broiler to reveal the steaks cooking there. "You got it," she laughed.

"I did." Regan opened the fridge door to reveal a bottle of wine she had also purchased. "To celebrate."

"Mmm," Lindy licked her lips. "Can we start on that now?"

"Wait until the steaks are ready."

Lindy sat down on one of the two bar stools they possessed. "What was Mr. Western like?" she asked eagerly.

"Very good-looking. Very charming, too!"

"Any chance of you and he—"

"Certainly not," Regan instantly denied, although the warmth in Clive Western's eyes had occasionally been a little too warm for comfort. A little encouragement from her, and who knows? Thank heavens he traveled a lot. It wouldn't do to become romantically involved with her employer.

Lindy shrugged. "Just curious. What's the little girl like?"

"She's a young lady," Regan corrected firmly. "I'm sure you didn't like being called a little girl at sixteen. And I didn't get to meet her—she's at their house in Cornwall. Apparently she lives there most of the time."

"Does that mean—"

"It means—" Regan checked the steaks once more, turning them over for the last time "—I will be going to Cornwall to live, and that Christopher will be able to move in here Sunday afternoon."

Lindy blushed. "Don't be like that, Regan. Christopher will be using your bedroom, not sharing mine. We only want to see how we get on living together. It isn't going to be easy to work a marriage around my shift work at the hospital."

Lindy was training to be a nurse, and her hours were a little strange, including several months of night work each year. She and Christopher McGrath had been dating for over a year now, and while Lindy's work didn't interfere too much when they were just going out together, it could be a different matter when taken in conjunction with the commitment of marriage. And so the young couple had decided to try living together for a while, with separate sleeping arrangements, to see how things worked out between them.

Regan kept an open mind about the idea, not sure she would want to do that herself. But then she had never been put to that sort of test, never caring enough for any of her boyfriends to want any more than a casual friendship with them. But she knew Lindy and Christopher genuinely cared for each other, and perhaps it was better to find any loopholes in the idea of marriage between them before they actually went ahead and did it.

Lindy frowned. "Sunday, you said? Is that when you start the job?"

She nodded. "Mr. Western is driving down to see his daughter and offered to take me with him. It will save me having to get a train."

"Bit short notice, though, isn't it."

Regan served their meal, sitting beside her friend at the breakfast bar. The two of them had shared an apartment ever since they had met in a youth hostel two years ago, and the arrangement had worked out very well, although after growing up with two male cousins, Regan had found it strange to suddenly be living with a female.

She shrugged now. "I've had a couple of weeks' break, and it isn't as if I can't start anytime. Besides, now I know I have the job I just want to get down to it."

"You're taking a risk not actually meeting this girl. She could turn out to be a little horror."

"Mr. Western more or less told me she is," Regan said calmly.

"Charming!"

"She just needs attention. She seems to have most things money can buy, but not too much tender loving care."

"Which you intend to rectify," Lindy teased.

"I'm going to try. Hey, we forgot the wine." She looked down ruefully at her already half-eaten meal.

"We'll have it now." Lindy got up to uncork it. "We have to toast your new job. Here." She handed Regan a full glass of the red wine. "Although I have to say you're a braver person than I am, I couldn't leave London for goodness knows how long."

"You forget, I was brought up in the country. Actually, I think that helped me get the job."

Lindy touched her glass to Regan's. "The new job," she toasted.

"The new job," Regan echoed.

"Does Donny know yet?"

Regan sighed. "Not yet. I'm dreading telling him, actually, although in a way I'll be glad to get away from him. He's got so possessive lately. I'm hoping to get out of this without too much fuss."

"Why not just tell him you aren't interested?"

"I tried that," Regan grimaced, carrying her wine through to their sitting room. "He just came around the next evening as if I hadn't said anything to him. I didn't have the heart to go through it all again."

Lindy curled up in a chair. "That's probably what he was counting on."

"Probably," she laughingly agreed. "But even he wouldn't follow me down to Cornwall."

"I wouldn't count on it. He hardly lets you out of his sight." The doorbell rang. "Now's your chance to find out."

"How can you be sure it's him?" Regan stood up.

"Simple. Chris isn't coming over until later."

"A process of elimination, Watson," she laughed.

She let Donny in, still not sure why she could only feel mild attraction toward him. He was good-looking enough—very tall, with the body of one of his own country's Greek gods, his hair deeply black, waving down in wild disorder to his shoulders, his eyes a deep brown, surrounded by thick black lashes. Regan knew that for work he wore smartly tailored suits—working for a shipping firm he had to look his best—but out of work he wore skin-tight jeans and T-shirts. He was a very good-looking individual of twenty-two...and yet he left her cold.

She accepted the kiss he placed on her lips, averting her face as he would have deepened the caress. She wished he would accept her friendship and not keep trying to make it something it could never be.

Lindy had gone to her bedroom by the time they entered the sitting room, no doubt to leave the field clear for Regan to tell Donny of her future change of location. As she had already known, he didn't like it, not one little bit.

"You will hate it there," he said angrily. "There will be no nightlife there, no parties, no discos. Just think of the fun we have here."

"To tell you the truth, the parties and discos have started to pall a bit. Whatever happened to moonlight walks and days spent by the river?"

His expression showed his disgust. "I can't imagine anything worse!" he groaned.

"Not here in London, no. Go for a moonlight walk and you're likely to get mugged, and the pollution of the river is likely to kill you if you get too close. I'm a country girl, Donny, and I'm looking forward to the move."

"And what about me?" he asked moodily. "You know what will happen to us if you move away from here."

"There is no *us*, Donny," she dismissed softly. "And as I told you, I want to go. I lived in London because I had to; now that I've finished college I would like to move back out again."

"You cannot tell me you will not miss all this," he scorned, his accent deepening in his anger. "I would go mad if I had to live in some quiet backwater."

"That's where we differ. I'm looking forward to it."

"You are determined to go?" He knew that stubborn look of old.

"Yes."

"All right," he sighed. "But remember this, I tried to stop you. You will remember that?"

She laughed. "I'll remember. And I'm sure to miss you."

"That is what I am hoping."

"Oh, I see," she nodded. "A case of absence making the heart grow fonder."

"Oh, Regan," his eyes pleaded. "I wish you would not go." He seemed about to say more and then checked himself. "I cannot stop you?" he said resignedly.

"No."

"Very well. As there are only a couple of days left before you are to leave, I intend showing you everything you are going to miss, starting tonight with a party one of the girls is throwing."

The next two days were a rush. When she wasn't out with Donny she was either packing or shopping. A lot of the clothing she had worn at college was not suitable to wear as a companion to an almost sixteen-year-old. Most of her things wouldn't set too good an example of neatness.

And then there was the call to her aunt and uncle, and their disappointment was immense when they knew she was moving even farther away from them. She was upset about that herself, being very close to them. In fact they had brought her up even before her father had died, her mother being Aunt Edith's younger sister. Regan's mother had died when she was seven, although she and her mother had often lived with Aunt Edith and Uncle Fred, as her father often was away.

When her mother had died, her aunt and uncle had stepped in to look after her, her father only putting in the occasional appearance. She had loved her father with a love akin to hero worship, had come to know him as the man who turned up for a day or two bearing gifts, and then disappeared again for six months or so. When he had suddenly died, and stopped appearing every now and then to disrupt the even tenor of her young life, she had for a few brief seconds felt a sense of relief. The guilt for that moment had never left her.

Finally Sunday morning came, bringing bright sunshine with it. Regan donned one of the new sundresses she had acquired, waiting anxiously for Clive Western to arrive. Lindy had only just gone to bed, her night shifts for this year just starting. Well, at least it would throw her and Christopher, who was moving in later today, in at the deep end. They were to have that test on their relationship straight away. Regan hoped it would work out for them.

Saying goodbye to Donny hadn't been easy, and she hoped he wasn't going to make a nuisance of himself in the near future. Mr. Western had seemed nice, but he may not consider Donny a suitable friend for the companion of his daughter.

When the doorbell rang at exactly nine o'clock, she knew it was him, and picked up her suitcase before taking one last look around what had been home to her for a long time now.

The drive was long and tiring, although the Mercedes was the ultimate in comfort. The powerful engine ate up the miles, and when the two of them weren't talking there was always the radio to fill in their silences. In actual fact Clive Western seemed to be becoming more and more preoccupied the closer to their destination they got, and with the heat of the day, the relaxing music and the comfort of her surroundings, Regan soon fell asleep.

She felt terrible when she woke up; she always did if she fell asleep during the day. She sat up, smoothing back her long hair, wishing now that she had combed it back in the style she had had at her interview. She must look a mess.

"Feeling better?" Clive Western turned to smile at her.

"A bit bedraggled," she admitted ruefully.

"I'll be stopping for gas in a minute; perhaps you would like to freshen up then."

Ten minutes later she felt grateful for his thoughtfulness, her face newly washed, her makeup renewed and her hair brushed. Ready to face anyone, in fact.

The house certainly was remote—a large gray bricked building set high on the cliff top, the only apparent habitation for several miles. There were several outbuildings, a couple of them looking like stables. She hoped so, for she would love to go riding once again. She hadn't been able to since her move to London, and it had been a pastime she particularly enjoyed.

Clive Western brought the car to a halt in the driveway at the front of the house, and after getting out Regan went to peer over the edge of the cliff to the sheer drop to the tumultuous blue gray sea below. The water looked icy cold—although in the heat of the day it probably wasn't—as it crashed against the jagged rocks that were scattered along the shoreline.

"Brr," she shivered, turning away to meet Clive Western's curious stare. "It doesn't look very inviting," she explained.

"It's very dangerous," he confirmed, taking her suitcase out of the trunk of the car. "I wouldn't advise that you attempt to swim in it. There's a pool at the back of the house. I would use that.''

"I think I will, thank you." She was perfectly well aware of how treacherous the Cornish coast could be; there were reports of deaths there every year. "I saw some stables, too—will I be allowed to use one of the horses?''

"You ride?" He sounded surprised.

Regan smiled. "I'm a country girl, remember?''

"Of course," he smiled back. "I can't see why you shouldn't ride one of the horses; they could probably do with the exercise.''

"Oh, lovely." Her eyes glowed deeply blue with her pleasure.

"Come into the house, Miss Thomas. I'm sure you're as ready for your lunch as I am. Mrs. Hall will take you up to your room first," he said as the housekeeper came out into the reception area to meet them. "I have to go to the office, but no doubt we will meet again later," he told Regan with a regretful smile. "Work has to come first, as usual," he grimaced.

Mrs. Hall was a rotund woman in her fifties, with a friendly welcoming smile on her lips, but her dignity demanding a certain respect. Regan knew that her job as companion could be a friendless one, not fitting in with the household staff and yet not a member of the family, either, but Mrs. Hall soon showed her there would be no resentment of her in any household she ran.

"Come along with me, my dear," Mrs. Hall invited in what must surely be a local accent. "Work, work, work," she shook her head. "These men seem to think of nothing else. Working in the office on a Sunday morning," she mumbled. "It wouldn't do for me, I'm sure.''

"I suppose Mr. Western is kept pretty busy," Regan said noncommittally, mentally thinking that Clive Western's time when he arrived would have been better spent saying hello to his young daughter.

"He is that," the housekeeper chuckled. "Kept on his toes, he is. Here we are." She opened a door, ushering Regan inside. She stood with her arms crossed over her bosom, looking with satisfaction about the scrupulously clean room. "I hope this is to your liking."

It was a beautiful room, the decor a range of different shades of mauve, from pale lilac to deep purple. Scatter cushions adorned the huge double bed, making it a comfortable place to rest during the day, too. Deep purple carpet, pale lilac bedspread, wallpaper comprising all the mauve shades imaginable—it was a lovely room, decorated with a woman's comfort in mind. There was even a range of perfumes on the dressing table, as well as an expensive-looking brush-and-comb set.

"Bathroom's through here." Mrs. Hall opened another door. "A private bathroom, of course," she added proudly, just as if she felt the house were really her own.

"It's lovely." And so much more than Regan had expected! But then with wealth like Clive Western's, she didn't suppose there was a less luxurious room that could be allocated to her.

"Good," the housekeeper beamed her pleasure. "Lunch will be in half an hour, but I'm sure you'll see the master before then. In the meantime, I'll get a refreshing pot of tea sent up."

"Thank you," Regan smiled shyly, feeling completely welcome—by the staff at least. "I'd like that."

She sat down on the bed once she was alone, hardly able to believe her good fortune, and looked around her in a dazed fashion. Her room and bathroom were truly beautiful; much too beautiful for a mere companion.

She only hoped Helena Western wouldn't prove too difficult. What little Clive Western had revealed of his daughter made Regan aware that she would have to be firm from the start. Any sign of weakness and she had no doubt her charge would take advantage of it.

Regan slipped off her shoes, taking off the jacket to her sundress, glad that the material hadn't creased. It was very warm in the room, and she moved to open the window, breathing deeply of the fresh sea air.

She jumped nervously at the sound of a tray banging onto a surface, and turned slowly to face Helena Western. She knew it had to be her, sure that no maid under Mrs. Hall's authority would dare to behave in such a manner.

"I apprehended the maid bringing you this," the young girl with flashing green eyes informed her coldly. "She should not be waiting on you. You are not wanted here," she said insultingly.

Yes, this was definitely Helena Western, although she must take after her mother in looks, for she had none of her father's fair coloring. Thick dark hair, almost black, cascaded in wild disorder halfway down her back. Those flashing green eyes, darkly olive skin, and a body that seemed to be growing too fast for her years, all made up the unruly adolescent Helena Western undoubtedly was. She would be a beautiful girl when she was older and more able to accept her femininity.

"I suppose you consider yourself above poor Mary," she continued resentfully. "Well, as far as I am concerned you rate far below the lowest servant here."

"Helena!" A hard voice rasped the girl's name in harsh disapproval, a husky male voice, the owner of which Regan couldn't yet see, he still being out in the corridor. "You will go to your room," he ordered. "Now!"

"But, papa," Helena protested. "I do not want this woman here, you know I do not." The defiance seemed to have gone out of her now.

Papa? Regan frowned. That voice, slightly accented, didn't belong to Clive Western. But then when had he ever said Helena was his daughter? Hadn't she just assumed that was the case? She waited apprehensively for her first sight of Helena's father. He didn't sound at all like the pleasant man Clive Western had proved to be on the journey down here.

"You will go to your room immediately," that harsh voice repeated. "I will not tell you again."

"Yes, papa." Helena turned to give Regan one last resentful glare before disappearing out of the room.

Regan's eyes widened as a man stepped into the open doorway, a tall man who seemed to block out most of the daylight in the room. He stepped forward and she was able to distinguish his features properly. What she saw made her face pale and then turn gray, her legs no longer feeling as if they would support her. He was the avenging angel from all her childhood nightmares, the man she had wished never to meet.

She would know that face anywhere—hadn't it haunted her for years, day and night? "Andreas Vatis..." she said faintly.

He gave a cruel smile. "Right first time, Miss... Matthews."

She sat down before she fell down, looking at Andreas Vatis like a mouse must look at a particularly cruel cat—before it ate it. That cruel hard face with the pencil-thin scar that ran from the bridge of his hawklike nose over his right eye and disappeared into the thick hair at his temple, black hair going gray over his ears. Green eyes looked at her contemptuously, with nothing to show that the scar and its internal injuries had rendered this man blind in his right eye; temporarily completely blind, but now having regained the sight of his left eye. The firm mouth was bared in a smile of taunting humor, his teeth very white against his naturally dark skin.

Regan had never met this man before, and yet she knew so much about him. A Greek to his fingertips, he had been a rakish hell raiser when the accident that had blinded him had taken place, an accident on the race

track that her father had also been involved in. It was
after this accident that her father had lived openly with
this man's estranged wife!

"My . . . my name is Thomas now," she informed him
tonelessly. "My aunt and uncle adopted me."

He nodded. "To save you the pain of your father's
sins," he grated. "But a simple change of name cannot
save you from me."

If anything she went even grayer, this man's expression frightening her. "Save me?"

"Yes," Andreas Vatis rasped. "I am a Greek, Regan
Matthews, and a Greek never forgets an insult or wrong
done to him. It may take years to attain retribution for
that wrong, but you can be sure we will always be
avenged on our sworn enemies."

Regan backed away from the glittering dislike in those
green eyes, still finding it difficult to believe he was half-
blind. He didn't appear to be a man who would have pa-
tience with any imperfection, although his harsh good
looks would never be forgotten by man or woman. How
had her father dared to take this man's wife from him?
By seeing him rendered blind first, that was how.

God, it still sickened her after all these years. Her
aunt and uncle had tried to keep the truth from her, but
they couldn't hide the fact that her father had taken this
man's wife from him when he was in no position to stop
him. Regan had learned of her father's behavior by
listening to her aunt and uncle talking when they
weren't aware she could hear.

Both race-car drivers, her father had seen Andreas
Vatis's wife and wanted her for himself. Of course Gina
Vatis must have been a very shallow woman to have
turned to the other man when it appeared her husband
was going to be blind for life, but as far as Regan was
concerned, her father had been the biggest offender
against the man. And now it appeared that Andreas
Vatis wanted revenge in some way.

She gulped. "I—I have nothing, no money, nothing," she told him desperately, although what this man would want with more money when he must be a millionaire time and time again she had no idea.

The Vatis family, of which Andreas was now the head, had always been in shipping, although Andreas had chosen to enjoy himself racing cars until the accident had made that impossible. In time he had taken over the family business, and according to Clive Western, they had now expanded into hotels and holiday accommodation.

Andreas Vatis threw back his head in a harsh laugh, the column of his thickly corded throat deeply brown, the cream silk shirt and cream trousers he wore emphasizing the slenderness of his waist and hips and the broadness of his muscular shoulders. He was a man in the peak of physical condition, much fitter than men half his thirty-five years. "I do not want money, Regan," he told her with a hard smile. "But you are right; I do want something. I want that which is mine by right."

She frowned. "But I don't have anything." She shook her head in puzzlement, feeling as if one of her nightmares were becoming a reality.

"On the contrary," he drawled. "You have everything that I want," he said softly, his gaze running over her appraisingly, almost insolent in its intensity. "I want only that which your father took from me."

She swallowed hard. "And that is?"

"A wife, Regan." His hard face was unyielding. "I am going to take *you* for my wife."

CHAPTER TWO

"No!" SHE GASPED. "You can't mean that!" She searched that cold hard face for some sign of mockery, but all she could see was his hatred and contempt of her.

"But I do mean it," he told her calmly. "I have waited almost eleven years for this moment. I cannot tell you how much it pleases me."

"But I—what does it all mean?" she demanded.

"It means that I have brought you here to become my wife, the wife your father chose to deprive me of," Andreas Vatis's voice taunted grimly. "I have never been particularly attracted to redheads," he added insultingly. "But then I will not be able to distinguish the color of your hair in the dark."

Regan gulped. "In the dark?" she echoed.

He nodded his arrogant head. "When I take you to my bed. Only the sense of touch is important at such times, and you look as if your body might be quite... pleasant to touch."

She blushed under his assessing gaze, feeling as if he stripped the clothes from her at a glance, saw each delectable curve beneath. "You're mad!" her voice quivered in her fear. "I'm not going to marry you, and you certainly aren't going to touch me, in the dark or at any other time."

"Are you sure of that?" He seemed unperturbed by her outburst, his calmness making Regan feel even more uneasy.

"Very sure." But her voice quivered uncertainly.

"Then I will keep you here until you change your

mind. Of course I will visit your bed every night until you agree to marry me, which should not be long. Helena was born exactly nine months after the consummation of my first marriage," he added with grim humor.

"You mean—"

"I mean that unless you agree to marry me now, you could find yourself in the even more unwelcome position, in your opinion, of being my mistress."

"But why?" she cried. "Why are you doing this to me?" Her anguish was obvious, her blue eyes shadowed.

"I have already explained it to you," he told her haughtily. "I want from your father the wife he stole from me, and as both he and Gina are dead, I intend taking his daughter instead. You will provide me with the sons I need to inherit the Vatis empire—the sons Gina would have given me if not enticed away by James Matthews, your father."

"But I—you got me here under false pretenses, didn't you," she accused. "You knew I would never have come here if I had known I was to be employed by Andreas Vatis. I'm only too aware of how you must hate me, and I wouldn't willingly come within a hundred miles of you. What I don't understand is how you arranged it all."

He shrugged his broad shoulders, walking over to study the perfumes she had so admired earlier. "It was all too easy, Regan. I have always known of your existence, of your adoption by your uncle and aunt, but as a child you were no good to me. Now you are a woman, a very beautiful one—"

"Except for the red hair," she cut in bitterly.

He looked at the waving tresses. "Perhaps I will come to like it in time. But as I said, it is not important that I do."

"Because you won't see it in the dark," she said

dully, a terrible feeling of inevitability washing over her. It was as if she had known for the past ten years that something like this was going to happen, that she wasn't really surprised by anything Andreas Vatis was saying to her.

"Exactly," he agreed cruelly. "But to get back to how I arranged this meeting." He picked up one of the bottles of perfume, smelling its fragrance. He grimaced, replacing it to pick up one of the others. "I have known of your every move since you were ten years old. I knew of your school friends, of your chosen career, of the friends you have made in London."

"What if I had become serious about one of these friends, had decided to marry one of them?"

"You almost did, did you not?" he inquired calmly. "A certain Rick Davidson. The romance—" he sneered the word "—broke up when you found him at his apartment with another girl."

"You've certainly done your homework," she snapped.

"Not at all. I have always found Diana very...obliging."

Regan's eyes widened. "You mean you arranged that, too?"

"It was not difficult, let me assure you. Diana liked Rick Davidson very much, and your boyfriend was only too willing. They are married now, you know. Since that time you have been escorted by a Donny Paulos."

"Don't tell me," she scorned. "You arranged that, too."

"It was necessary," Andreas Vatis told her coldly.

"You mean you *did* arrange it?" she gasped.

"Certainly. I felt it safer to put you in the care of one of my employees rather than risk you becoming seriously involved again. Of course, he had no idea of my reason for wanting you watched."

So this was the reason Donny refused to be shaken off. "That's disgusting!"

"Perhaps," he conceded with a nod of his head. "But I do not want anything but a virgin in my bed. You are to know only my possession."

She met his gaze challengingly. "And how can you be so sure that I haven't been to bed with Donny? He's very attractive," she added tauntingly.

"But aware of his own vulnerability. If he has laid one finger on you that I would class as intimate, I will break him. I will make sure he never works again, that all his friends suddenly forget his existence, that his family—"

"Okay, okay, I think you've made your point," she said miserably.

His eyes narrowed to icy green slits. "Did he touch you?"

"Frequently," she answered flippantly.

"Intimately?" he demanded to know.

She shrugged. "It depends what you call intimate. We all have our own definition. And my idea of intimate may differ from yours."

He took a threatening step toward her, his strong fingers biting painfully into her arm. "You will answer me!" he ordered. "Did he touch you like this?" His other hand came up to cup one of her breasts through the thin material of her blouse, caressing until he felt the nipple harden to full arousal. "Or like this?" The hand moved to her thighs, moving exploratively over her silky skin. "Did he?" he demanded grimly, his fingers digging into the tender flesh of her thighs.

It was so tempting to say yes; Donny *had* betrayed her after all. But she didn't doubt that Andreas Vatis would indeed break him, and she wasn't sure he deserved that, for all his deceit. Besides, when he had known of her plans he had tried to stop her. Perhaps he had realized her fate!

"No, he never touched me like that." No man had. She was ashamed of her own response to this man's hands on her body, her breasts still tingling from his touch.

"Nor any other man?" he persisted harshly.

"Nor any other man," she admitted dully. No one else had ever induced her to such sexual excitement!

He released her so suddenly she almost fell, he seemingly unmoved by the way he had just touched her, moving back to study the perfumes as if he had never deviated his attention from them. "When you finished your college course I contacted the employment agency you went to and asked for you to be sent for an interview."

"To Clive Western. Is he in on this, too?" she asked disgustedly.

"Clive employed you on my instructions, but he did not know the real reason I wanted you here. I think he perhaps imagined I had another relationship in mind."

"So Helena doesn't need a companion?"

"As her stepmother I expect you to become just that. Your duties as my wife will not be too arduous. . .during the daytime hours."

Regan glared at him. "I've already told you I'm not going to marry you."

Andreas Vatis shrugged. "That is your choice, of course. Here." He handed her one of the perfumes. "Wear this tonight when I come to your room."

"I won't be here tonight. I'm leaving."

"I think not," he removed the key to the room, placing it on the outside of the door, his intention clear. "And we are three floors up. I would not recommend you jump," he mocked.

"But you can't keep me here against my will," she told him desperately.

"I am not doing that, *you* are. As my wife you will be

perfectly free to go where you choose . . . within reason.
As my mistress—''

"Don't you mean sex slave?" she scorned.

"I require sons from you. Unfortunately they cannot
be obtained without the sexual act."

"You're inhuman!"

"But you are not," he smiled tauntingly. "You liked
my hands upon you just now. Do not deny it. I am not
ignorant of the workings of a woman's body. I know
pleasure when I see it. And you liked what I did to you.
Tonight there will be more; much more," he promised
mockingly.

"No!" her voice came out shrill.

His eyes narrowed. "Does that mean you will marry
me?"

"No." She shook her head firmly.

He shrugged. "Then you will wear the perfume tonight. It is called Desirable. Let us hope I find you that
way by tonight."

Regan was aware that he was insulting her again, that
his words were designed to cause humiliation. "You
can't get away with this sort of thing in this country,"
she informed him tautly. "It's called kidnapping. And
rape will be added to that if you carry out your threat."

"You came here of your own free will. I have witnesses to the fact."

"But I'm not staying from the same freedom."

"In a few weeks' time you will not want to leave," he
told her with indifference. "I will make sure of that."

"You're doing all this because of what happened ten
years ago?"

His mouth tightened. "Yes."

"And if I agree to marry you?"

"Then you will be shown every consideration."

"Except that I would still have to share your bed."

"Unless you know of some other way we can have
children." His smile was cruelly mocking.

She took a deep breath. "All right, I'll marry you."

His green eyes narrowed questioningly, his intent gaze searching her features. Regan forced herself to remain calm. "You are up to something," he said slowly, suspiciously. "Do you think by agreeing you will encourage me to let you roam freely around the estate? Do you take me for a fool, Regan? You will remain in your room until tomorrow. I have arranged for us to be married then."

"You were so sure of me," she said bitterly.

"You have no real choice," he told her arrogantly.

Oh, yes, she did, and one he wasn't aware of. she hadn't been a tomboy for nothing. Once Andreas Vatis had left her room, she intended climbing down the drainpipe she had seen outside her window—something she had done a lot as a child—and escaping. "Does that mean that you'll leave me alone tonight?"

"Poor Regan, are you afraid of being in a man's arms?" he taunted.

"Not a man's," she flushed. "But the devil's, yes."

"So I am the devil now, am I?" he rasped, obviously not liking what she said. "Then make sure you do not bring out the devil in me when I possess you," he warned. "I could hurt you very much."

He would never possess her, never! "Will you have my lunch sent up here?"

He looked taken aback, finally giving a husky laugh. "I will never understand the workings of a woman's mind; her body, yes, but never her mind. One minute we are talking of sharing a bed, the next you are talking of food."

Because her mind was racing on to her escape, to gaining the most time before it was discovered she had gone, and she needed to know whether a maid would be coming up here in the next hour or so. "They're both appetites," she dismissed. "At the moment I happen to consider the latter of more importance. And you probably don't understand a woman's mind, because that has never been the part of a woman you're interested in." She knew he kept a low profile on his affairs, but she also knew there had to have been several. The experience of his hands hadn't been carried forward ten years from his wife. Besides, he emitted a sexual aura that under any other circumstances she may have been drawn to. But never through force or under duress!

"You are probably right." He didn't rise to her taunt. "And yes, your lunch will be sent up here. I dare not risk you seeing Clive and trying to convince him to take you back to London with him. He is loyal to me, but he also has a strong sense of what is wrong and what is right."

"And he would know this is wrong!"

"I'm afraid so." He nodded.

She was more and more convinced her plan was going to work. Once she had climbed down the drainpipe she could stow away in the back of Clive's car. There was a blanket on the back seat she could cover herself with, and he had said he would be leaving shortly after lunch. If she timed this right she shouldn't have to be cramped on the back seat for long. Once away from here she was sure she could convince Clive of Andreas Vatis's ruthless plan to slake his revenge on her.

"Then you admit it," she accused.

"I admit that to an Englishman what I am doing would not be thought...gentlemanly," he sneered the word. "But I do not consider it gentlemanly of one man to try to kill another, either. Oh, yes," he said grimly as she made to protest, "your father did not intend to blind or even maim me when he forced me off the race circuit; he intended to kill."

Regan was once again deathly pale. "I don't believe you." She shook her head in denial of his words. "My father—"

"Was a very dangerous man. He thought that by kill-ing me he would be free to marry Gina. But we Vatises do not die so easily. I was very badly injured—''

"I know," she put in quietly. "I...I saw a report of the crash."

"So," he nodded. "Both my legs and one arm were broken, several ribs also, one of which punctured a lung. But none of these things mattered to me in comparison with the taking of my sight. That I could never forgive." His mouth twisted bitterly. "Gina could take none of it, and I admit I was not a sight to please the eyes of a woman, not even the woman who had sworn before God to love me for all time. Gina went to visit her parents and she did not come back. Your father had arranged to meet her there, deciding that it would have to be a divorce, after all. There was only one thing he did not take into account, and that was that I would still not divorce Gina. I do not believe in it."

"My father loved your wife. He...he wanted to marry her. I don't believe he would harm anyone to get what he wanted."

"Considering he was no father to you, I am surprised you still feel it necessary to defend him," Andreas Vatis scorned.

"I'm not defending him—I'm saying you're wrong about him. My father would never deliberately hurt anyone, let alone try to kill them."

"But I have witnesses, Regan."

She had gone very pale. "W-witnesses?"

"Of course," he nodded haughtily. "You are not listening to the ramblings of a demented man," he snapped. "Shortly before the race in which I was injured, your father and I had an argument. He wanted me to divorce Gina, and when I refused he threatened to kill me."

"The words of an angry man." She remembered her father's explosive temper well, his nature as fiery as the red lights in his hair.

"I do not think so. And neither did the other five drivers who heard him say it. While I lay unconscious in my hospital bed an inquiry into the accident was taking place—privately, of course. It would not do to cast aspersions on a man's character until they were sure. If I had not been unconscious I could have told them that your father deliberately swerved in front of me." His harsh features were frightening in their anger.

"And the . . . the inquiry?" she hardly dared to ask.

His dark gaze leveled on her. "It was dropped."

"There you are, then," she said triumphantly. "You must be mistaken."

"I am not mistaken. Strange, is it not, that your father retired from racing after that race? A few months later he was dead."

"And you've been planning this revenge all those years."

"Oh, yes. I told you, it may take a long time, but a Greek never forgives or forgets."

"So it seems," she said dully, putting a hand up to her aching temple. "I—I would like to lie down. I'm not feeling well."

"Poor Regan," he taunted. "What a shock for you."

"Sh-shock?"

"To come here thinking you are simply starting a new job when in fact you are to become my wife. A dutiful one, I hope."

"Never!" her eyes flashed at him. "I don't intend being meek, in bed or out of it."

His green eyes sparkled with interest. "I will like that. Yes, I will like that. But you must understand that your position as my wife will not be the ordinary one."

"I already know that," she scoffed. "You've made your feelings very clear."

"I do not think so." He shook his head. "In Greece a wife is revered above all other women, respected as the mother of our children. We have our . . . friends, that is accepted, but the wife always comes first. Gina had that place in my life and she abused my trust of her. You will not be given the same consideration.''

"Oh, I see, your *friend* will come first.''

"I believe I said *friends*, and that is exactly what I meant. You will provide me with my sons, and I will get my pleasure elsewhere.''

"My God, you *are* inhuman.''

"I think you will find I am human,'' he corrected. "If you learn to please me you may even find I can be *very* human. I may even forget my friends and stay in my wife's bed if I find you pleasing enough.''

"You can go to hell for all I care!''

He smiled mockingly. "Isn't that where the devil belongs?''

"Go away,'' she choked. "Go away and leave me alone!''

"I intend to. But I will lock the door, so that you will not be...tempted to try to escape.''

She heard the key turn in the lock immediately after he had closed the door. My God, he would pay for this! As soon as she was free and far away from here she would tell the police about him. The man had to be insane!

How could she have guessed when she had left London so happily this morning that this man would be behind it all, the man who even ten years ago had frightened her. There had been several photographs of him in the newspapers at the time of the accident, the crash that he claimed her father had deliberately caused, and just a photograph of his harsh features had been enough to frighten her. In the flesh he was even more daunting, and his intention of becoming her husband, in every sense, terrified the life out of her.

Could he be right about her father's involvement in his accident? Could he really have meant to kill Andreas Vatis? She had seen her father furiously angry only once in her life, when he had struck her uncle to the ground. But murder? She didn't believe he was capable of that, no matter what Andreas Vatis said to the contrary.

She jumped nervously as the key turned in the lock once more, forgetting Andreas Vatis's promise to provide her with lunch. Perhaps she wouldn't need to climb down the drainpipe after all—surely a maid wouldn't lock her back in this room? Her hopes were dashed as Andreas Vatis himself entered with the luncheon tray.

He smiled at her disappointment. "You did not expect me to make it possible for you to appeal to one of my staff?" He quirked an eyebrow mockingly. "Really, Regan, you surprise me. I am well aware that until you are actually my wife no one, if they knew of our past connection, would believe you are staying here through choice. Until after the ceremony tomorrow you will see only me."

"Won't your staff think that a little odd?"

"My staff have already been acquainted with the fact that my fiancée is feeling unwell."

She swallowed hard. "Your. . .your fiancée?"

"Did you not realize that everyone here believes us to be engaged to be married?" He shrugged. "With the haste of the wedding it was necessary to tell them this."

He had it all worked out, had covered every loophole! It had never occurred to her that Mrs. Hall believed her to be her employer's future bride. Only Clive Western knew the truth, and he was leaving after lunch!

Andreas Vitas laughed at her expression of dismay, a soft mocking laugh that taunted. "I have been planning this for years, Regan. You have only known an hour or so. You would be advised to admit defeat, and stop fighting me."

"I'll fight you to hell and back!"

"Tomorrow night I'll take you there," he promised cruelly. "Your father put me there for two years, took away my sight and made me a prisoner of my hatred for him and his family. When I came out of the darkness I determined to take you there one day."

"But I can't be blamed for what my father did or didn't do." She despised herself for her almost pleading tone. This man was granite, pure granite, and no amount of pleading on her part would change his mind about her, so she might as well save her breath. "I hardly ever saw him. I never had any life with him; he was always too busy. And his career didn't allow for a child tagging along behind him."

"I know that," this tall Greek said arrogantly. "It is because of your early removal from your father's influence that I feel able to offer you marriage—"

"*Offer* me marriage?" she repeated in amazement. "I don't remember there being any question about it. You *told* me I was to marry you."

"I seem to remember I gave you an alternative."

"Of being your mistress or your wife! What a choice," she scorned.

She knew she had gone too far by the white ring of anger around his firm, forbidding mouth and his suddenly cold eyes. She hadn't realized before how alive with feeling his eyes were, how reflective of his mood they could be. Right now they showed his burning anger.

"You little bitch!" he spat out, looming up in front of her, his hands moving out and shaking her. "Do you think I enjoy being like this! That I like being half blind? My God, I hate it! But being half blind does not make me half a man, as you are about to find out," he finished grimly.

"No—" Her protest was cut off by the brutal assault of his mouth on hers, forcing her lips savagely apart with the tip of his tongue, devouring her until she was senseless.

He was all demand, all aroused male as he pushed her down on the bed before covering her with his body. He held her hands pinned above her head with one of his as she tried to fight free of him.

"No, please..." she cried her fear of the determination clearly written in his face.

"Oh, yes," he grated. "Only this way will you learn that I am the master here, that you will obey my will and no other." His free hand came up to clasp the top of her sundress, pulling downward with complete disregard for the material. Several of the buttons came off altogether and the others easily parted from their openings, leaving her breasts clearly visible through the lacy cream material of her bra.

"Andreas!" she pleaded with him in spite of herself, but saw no softening of the anger in that harsh face. If only he would release her hands.... "Let me go," she begged.

"Soon you will beg to stay in my arms," he rasped. "Soon you will be oblivious of all but me," he promised grimly, tearing aside the thin lace of her bra to release her breasts to his avid gaze. "I had thought in this day and age that women no longer bothered with such a needless article of clothing." He showed his impatience with the lacy garment by ripping it even further. "With a body such as this you certainly do not need it." All the time he was talking he was caressing her creamy skin, watching the emotions that flitted across her face, smiling his pleasure as she seemed to lose control. He bent his head to her breasts, laughing softly as she groaned.

Regan felt as if she were drowning, a tide of emotion sweeping over her body and making her feel dizzy. She felt hot and cold at one and the same time; wanted to be free and yet wanted him to continue with his lovemaking, wanted, wanted—

Suddenly he was no longer with her on the bed but had moved to stand in front of her as someone entered the room.

"Mrs. Hall." He seemed relieved, moving aside to

reveal Regan's disheveled appearance. "I thought it was Helena," he explained. "And I am afraid that after such a long separation from my fiancée I became lost to all sensibility."

Regan had pulled the folds of her dress together, finding herself unable to look at the housekeeper. How damning this looked! How could she have let herself respond to the devil? Oh, she knew she couldn't have stopped him—he was much too strong for her to have done that—but did she have to respond to him? And he knew exactly what effect he had had on her, she could see he did by the mockery in his eyes as he turned to look at her.

Mrs. Hall looked a little taken aback, but she soon had her expression under control. "I just came up to make sure Miss Thomas has everything she needs," she said primly.

Andreas gave a wolfish smile, more relaxed than Regan had ever seen him. "I think she has everything she could possibly want," he said humorously, casting a triumphant smile in her direction.

The housekeeper allowed a smile to lighten her expression. "Yes, I suppose she has. I'm sorry I interrupted you."

"I think it as well that you did." Andreas walked to the door with her. "If you had not I may have been tempted to anticipate my wedding night, and that would never do. I am sure both Regan and I thank you."

Mrs. Hall noticed the luncheon tray. "Would you like me to get you something else for your lunch, Miss Thomas? I'm sure this will be cold by now."

"I—"

"Miss Thomas is not feeling well," Andreas cut in smoothly. "She does not feel like eating, do you, darling?" His mocking gaze dared her to disagree.

Regan cowed beneath that look. "No," she confirmed. "I'm afraid I'm feeling rather sick." The look she directed at Andreas Vatis left him in no doubt as to what had caused this nausea. She knew by the tightening of his mouth and the clenching of his hands into fists at his side that he had got her silent message.

If only it were true that he had made her feel sick with his touch, but it was disgust with herself that had done that. How could she have responded to a man who had accused her father of attempted murder and seemed set on forcing her to replace the wife her father had taken from him? She was shocked and dismayed at her reaction to this . . . this devil with the glittering green eyes.

"Perhaps a pot of tea or coffee?" the housekeeper persisted.

"No, I— Thank you, but I think I'll just lie down." If she didn't soon get out of here Clive Western would be on his way back to London without her safely hidden in the back of the car. "Could I do that?" she asked pointedly.

"But of course, my dear." Andreas Vatis moved to the door. "Mrs. Hall and I will leave you now. I will come back later to make sure you are not feeling any worse." That was a threat, not a promise.

She glared her dislike of him. "Thank you," she said between tight lips.

He smiled at her, a mocking smile that made her even angrier. "Rest now, Regan." His words seemed to imply she was going to need it.

She waited until she heard the sound of the key turning in the lock before going over to the window. Goodness, it was a long way down! Come to think of it, it was a long time since she had climbed even a tree, and a drainpipe certainly didn't have the footholds of a tree. Still, there was no other way she was going to get out of here before tomorrow, before her wedding. My God, if that wasn't incentive enough to climb down ten floors, let alone three, she didn't know what was! Especially when the proposed bridegroom was Andreas Vatis.

Just what sort of person did he think she was that she would meekly accept being forced into a marriage with a man who made no secret of his hatred of her? Well, whatever he thought, he was wrong; there was nothing meek about her, and never would be.

She changed into jeans and a sleeveless blouse for her climb. She would have to get out on the ledge first, as the nearest drainpipe was a couple of feet away. Getting out onto the ledge was easy enough, but after that it wasn't quite so easy. A look down at the ground made her knees shake. It certainly was a long way down! If she should fall...!

God, that just didn't bear thinking about. She made sure her balance was right before reaching out for the pipe, found it was farther away than she had thought, and had to make a grab for it at the last moment. It gave a terrific groan as it took the whole of her weight, but didn't seem to be loosened at all. Its fastenings to the wall were her only footholds, and now that she was actually on it, it was difficult to stop herself from falling.

It was a slow climb down, but she seemed to be making it. All she had to do when she reached the ground was—

"My God!" she heard a male voice rasp beneath her. "What do you think you are doing, Regan?"

She looked down over her shoulder; the ground seemed to spin dizzily beneath her. Andreas Vatis—it could only have been her tormentor—stood on the gravel driveway looking up at her, those luminous green eyes incredulous.

She looked back at the wall, trying to stop the sudden spinning of the world. She was still about twelve feet from the ground, out of arm's reach and yet too far from her bedroom window to climb back. So much for her certainty that she would be able to climb down without a hitch!

"What does it look like?" she asked through gritted teeth.

"You are either very stupid or very brave," he ground out angrily.

"Or just desperate," she said shakily.

"Come down from there," he ordered. "Now!"

"What do you think I'm trying—" That angry look around at him was her undoing. Everything started to spin once again, and at the same time her left foot slipped from its precarious perch. "Oh, no!" she had time to cry before she began to fall.

The ground suddenly wasn't twelve feet away anymore; it was painfully close. And she lay upon it like a broken doll.

CHAPTER THREE

AFTER THAT FIRST MOMENT OF IMPACT Regan prayed for
oblivion, but it was not to be. She had tried to land on
her feet, a natural reaction, and the pain that shot
up her leg from her ankle was excruciating. Her legs
buckled beneath her and she landed with a crash on her
left shoulder, the gravel cutting into her bare skin.

Andreas Vatis was at her side in seconds, turning her
over to face him, his anger evident by the grim tautness
around that firm mouth. "You stupid child!" He took
hold of her shoulders and shook her. "You stupid,
stupid child!"

"My shoulder!" she cried, her face paling even more.
"Oh, God, Andreas, please don't do that." She tried to
push his hand away from her bruised and ragged flesh.

His hand came away covered in blood, and he gave an
impatient exclamation before bending down to swing
her up into his arms. "Surely you were not so desperate
to escape my arms that you would rather die?" he
rasped curtly.

"Yes," she groaned against his chest, aware, even in
her pain, of the warm male smell of him, of the fine mat
of dark hair against her cheek. "I...I wanted to get
away," she admitted.

Several people came out into the reception area as
they entered the house—Mrs. Hall, Clive Western and
Helena Vatis. Regan had expected the latter to look
jubilant at her discomfort, but instead she just looked
resentful of her being in Andreas's arms. If only she
knew how Regan hated this closeness to him.

"Miss Thomas!" Mrs. Hall was all concern. "Whatever have you done to yourself?"

"Regan was out walking and tripped and fell," Andreas answered for her. "So the effort to clear your nausea has only caused you more pain." There was a double meaning for only Regan to read. "Call Peters," he instructed the housekeeper. "I will take Regan back to her room."

To her cell! And by the throbbing of her ankle and shoulder she didn't think she would be making any more escapes in the near future. Tears of pain and frustration flooded her eyes, and she bit her bottom lip to stop its trembling.

Andreas must have noticed the sudden shaking of her body because his arms tightened around her, causing her to gasp in pain. "I am sorry," he muttered as he felt her flinch. "But do not cry here."

Her blue eyes flashed. "I wasn't going to," she snapped vehemently.

"Regan, er, Miss Thomas," Clive Western amended at a look of disapproval from his employer. "Are you all right?"

"Of course she is not all right!" Once again Andreas Vatis answered for her. "Is it not obvious that she is hurt?"

The other man flushed. "Well, yes. But—"

"Then do not ask meaningless questions," Andreas dismissed impatiently.

Helena stepped forward, grasping her father's arm to stop him as he would have walked straight past her. "Papa," she said in a soft pleading voice. "Is it really necessary for you to carry Miss Thomas? Can she not walk?"

"That question is as meaningless as Clive's," her father snapped impatiently. "I would not be carrying her if she could walk. Now would you all get out of my way so that I might get Regan to her room before she faints."

She was surprised he had noticed, with all the other people demanding his attention, that for her the world had suddenly started to recede, a black fog starting to rise up in front of her. And Andreas had realized this, was acting upon it, finally taking her up the stairs.

"The key," he said abruptly as they stood outside the bedroom door. "Can you get it out of my trousers pocket? The left one."

She had forgotten the door was still locked. No wonder he had deterred anyone from coming up here with them. They would know his explanation of her going for a walk was a lie if they knew she couldn't possibly have left this room by the door.

Color flooded her cheeks. "Can't you reach it?"

He raised his eyes heavenward. "I seem to be surrounded by imbeciles today. Of course I cannot reach it. I only have one pair of hands, and at the moment they seem to be taken up with holding you."

"Then put me down." She began to struggle in his arms.

"Can you stand?" he demanded to know.

"No." The pain in her ankle told her that she couldn't.

"Then get the key. Come on, Regan," he encouraged angrily. "I cannot continue to hold you forever."

The strength in his arms told her that he may not be able to hold her forever, but he could certainly hold her for a very long time. But she really had no other choice than to get the key, embarrassing as the experience might be.

Luckily it didn't take her long. She heard Andreas Vatis let out a breath as she produced the key. "Do you want me to open the door?" She couldn't look at him.

"Give it to me." He held out his hand for it, managing, with some difficulty, to unlock the door. "I do not think you should use that arm until the doctor has looked at it."

"The doctor?" She looked startled as he put her on top of the bed. "You've sent for a doctor?"

He came back from the bathroom with a damp sponge soaked in antiseptic. "Who did you think Peters was?" He bent over her cut arm, gently removing some gravel that still remained in the cuts.

Regan drew a ragged breath. "I di-didn't know." She tensed as she felt the warm sponge on her arm, involuntarily moving away.

"Stay still," Andreas directed grimly. "This is a mess," he muttered angrily.

"I know," she agreed shakily.

"Whatever possessed you to do such a thing?" His lids raised and he looked at her with those startling green eyes.

"I told you. I wanted to get away."

"And instead you have made your position here even worse."

"W-worse?" she echoed.

"Mmm." His attention was back on her arm. "I noticed that your ankle is already swollen. I do not think you will be walking anywhere on it for some time."

She knew that, damn him! She lay back on the pillow, not caring anymore that he was hurting her arm and shoulder by washing it. "I hate you," she told him dully.

"I would not expect anything else." He stood back to survey her torn flesh. "That is going to be painful for some time to come."

Regan looked at him with tears in her eyes, and they weren't all because of her injuries. "It's painful now."

He shook his dark head with barely concealed impatience. "It was a stupid and impetuous thing to do and—"

"Okay," she cut into his angry tirade. "I'm stupid and impetuous. I think that's already been established."

Andreas moved to stand in front of the window, the sunlight making his slightly curly hair seem blacker than ever. "What did you hope to achieve? You would not have got very far even if you had got to the ground unharmed. As soon as I had discovered your room was empty I would have come after you. And I would have found you."

She knew that now, knew that wherever she went this man would follow and bring her back.

"I have not waited all these years for you to grow up to be put off by a little opposition," he continued haughtily, his thumbs hooked into the low waistband of the cream jeans he wore.

"A little opposition!" she repeated scornfully. "I can assure you it will be more than a little. How would you feel if someone was just waiting for your daughter to grow up so that he might be avenged on her?" she challenged.

"If I had done what your father did then I would expect such retribution."

And he meant it—she saw a cold acceptance in that harsh face. "Then you can't love your daughter."

His mouth tightened ominously. "I love Helena very much, never doubt that. If you ever do or say anything to hurt her you will answer to me."

"Does she know we're getting married?"

"She knows." He nodded distantly. "She would not show such resentment for a mere companion."

"And doesn't she think it strange that you're marrying someone she's never met before?"

Andreas shrugged. "It is not so strange in my country."

"But we aren't in Greece," Regan flared up. "And I'm not Greek."

"When you become my wife you will be so. I myself only live in Greece a few months out of every year. The rest of the time I spend traveling to the various Vatis branches, but I owe my allegiance to Greece, and I was brought up to be a Greek. You will learn the obedience of my countrywomen."

"I will not! I'm English and I'll remain so."

"We shall see," he told her coldly, his eyes narrowed. "Tomorrow you will become my wife, and if you ever attempt to leave me then I will follow you and bring you back. I would follow you to the ends of the earth if I had to. Understood?"

"Yes," she acknowledged dully, feeling as if a noose had just tightened around her throat.

"But you will have no need to fear me for some time," he mocked her. "I would not subject an injured woman to my lovemaking."

She inwardly sighed her relief, although she remained outwardly calm. "Really? Then perhaps I should just keep making sure I'm hurt," she taunted.

He smiled, his teeth very white against his dark skin. "That excuse will not last forever. And perhaps it is better this way. You will be my wife and never know when the time has come for me to claim my rights as your husband. I will enjoy seeing the torment you suffer as you wonder each day if it is to be the one." His smile was deliberately cruel. "As I wondered each day whether I would ever regain my sight," he added tautly. "Two years I suffered, Regan. I will try to make sure your torment does not last that long."

"The pleasure of not sharing your bed can last a lifetime as far as I'm concerned," she snapped.

There was cruelty in his grasp as he swung her around to look at him. "A few days, no more," he warned. "And now you will behave as my fiancée should. I have just seen the doctor arrive and no doubt Mrs. Hall will bring him in here in a moment.''

"And what if I tell him what you're doing to me? What then?'' she challenged.

He laughed, a taunting sound, deep and husky, and very attractive. "He will think you are suffering from shock and sedate you.''

"No, he won't, not if I tell him the truth. That you got me here under false pretenses, that you—''

Andreas shook his head. "It will not work, Regan. You see, the good doctor knows, as does everyone else in the district, that I have been visiting my fiancée in London for the last six months. He will put your distress down to wedding nerves.''

"But Clive Western knows the truth,'' she said shrilly. "He knows—''

"He will be leaving in five minutes, Regan. Leaving the house even while you tell Dr. Peters this strange tale. And this evening he will be on a flight back to Athens.''

"*Back* to Athens?''

"Clive runs my Greek office,'' he informed her calmly.

"I don't believe you,'' she cried. "You're lying to me! You—''

Her words were cut off by his mouth being forcibly placed on hers. It wasn't a kiss meant to be enjoyed or even to evoke a response, just a way of silencing her, as she realized a few seconds later when Mrs. Hall and the doctor appeared in the open doorway. God, this man didn't miss a trick. He must have heard the approach of the housekeeper and doctor, and by silencing her in this way he had also given the doctor the impression that she was quite prepared to accept his kisses. The other man would never believe her now if she tried to tell him she was being kept here against her will.

Andreas straightened, a look of triumph in his eyes

before he turned to face the newcomers to the room.
"James—" he put out his hand to the doctor "—I'm
glad you could come so promptly. As you can see,
Regan has been hurt." He brought the other man over
to the side of the bed. "That will be all, Mrs. Hall." He
dismissed her with a smile.

"Mr. Western wanted—"

"Tell him I will be down in a moment." His tone was
abrupt. "I cannot leave my fiancée at such a time."

"Yes, sir."

Regan looked at the doctor as he examined her arm.
She was sure if she could just get rid of Andreas she
could persuade this elderly man to believe her. He was a
middle-aged fatherly figure, portly, with graying brown
hair and twinkling blue eyes. She felt sure he would
listen to her...if only she could get rid of Andreas
Vatis!

She turned to the haughty Greek with a glowing
smile, her hand resting intimately on his arm. "I'll be
perfectly all right, Andreas," she told him huskily.
"You mustn't neglect your work because of me. I'm
sure you want to see Clive before he leaves."

Humor lightened his eyes, a mocking humor that told
her he knew exactly what she was up to. "Your health is
more important to me than anything I might have to say
to Clive." He took her hand to his lips, kissing her palm
intimately, his eyes full of devilment.

Regan's fingers clenched, and she would have pulled
her hand away if he had not retained such a tight grip on
it. "But you must say goodbye to him, Andreas," she
insisted silkily. "You know he has to leave in a few
minutes."

He shrugged his broad shoulders. "Then he will leave
without seeing me. I could not leave you now, not
when—" He broke off as she gasped, the doctor gently
probing her swollen ankle. "Is that broken, James?" he
spoke to the other man.

"I don't think so," James Peters shook his head. "Of course, an X ray could tell us better."

"Then she must have one," Andreas told him haughtily.

"I think so." The doctor frowned. "Mrs. Hall said your fiancée had tripped and fallen. This ankle doesn't look as if it's been twisted. It looks—"

"It was my fault, I am afraid," Andreas smoothly interrupted him. "Regan and I—" He paused for effect. "I had Regan in my arms and I dropped her."

The doctor looked even more puzzled. "Dropped her?"

"I have not seen Regan for some days and I am afraid our reunion got a little...heated," Andreas explained patiently. "I picked her up, swung her around...and dropped her."

"Oh, I see." The doctor looked uncomfortable now. "That would account for it," he mumbled.

Would it, indeed! Regan glared her dislike at the smug-looking Andreas Vatis. How dare he humiliate her like this in front of the doctor, to imply that they had been making love out in the driveway for all to see.

The examination over under the watchful eyes of Andreas Vatis, her shoulder was bandaged and her arm put in a sling because of the excessive bruising, a cold compress on her ankle and a card to have it x-rayed at the local hospital. She had pills for the pain in case she couldn't sleep, and her body felt as if she had had all eleven members of a football team trampling over it.

"I realize you aren't feeling in the mood at the moment," the doctor sympathized. "But I don't think you should wait until tomorrow to get that ankle looked at."

"We cannot leave it until tomorrow, anyway," Andreas informed him arrogantly. "Regan and I are to be married in the morning."

James Peters looked startled. "Married? Here, you mean?"

Andreas nodded. "Of course."

"I wouldn't advise Miss Thomas to do any traveling with her injuries. If her ankle isn't broken, it's very severely bruised and will need resting, not being walked on."

"We are not traveling anywhere, James. We will be spending our honeymoon here."

"Oh, I see." The other man nodded. "I didn't realize congratulations were in order." He beamed at them both.

Congratulations! Regan almost groaned out loud, could have screamed her frustration of being at Andreas Vatis's mercy. How could anyone imagine she would want to marry this arrogant devil of a man of her own free will.

"Dr. Peters—"

"I am sure we have taken up enough of your time for one day, James," Andreas cut in firmly. "You must be eager to return to your family."

"Not particularly," the doctor grimaced. "My daughter and her husband arrived just before lunch, and as she's expecting our first grandchild, she and my wife can talk of nothing but babies."

Andreas smiled his sympathy. "I hope you will honor us by being present at the birth of our first child."

James Peters's cheeks colored a ruddy hue. "I didn't realize...."

"I'm not pregnant!" Regan protested indignantly, her movement jarring her shoulder and causing her to go pale. "Andreas—"

"Of course you are not," he calmed her tauntingly. "I was referring to the fact that we intend to start a family straight away, to provide Helena with many brothers and sisters."

Regan's mouth set angrily. She had no intention of providing Helena with one brother or sister, let alone many!

"I do not want you to have other children, papa!" Helena Vatis launched herself into the room, apparently having listened unnoticed to their conversation. "And especially by *her*! I do not like her, papa," she sobbed against her father's chest.

"You will calm yourself, Helena," he ordered harshly, holding her at arm's length. "And you will apologize to Regan for this outburst."

"No!" Her green eyes, so like his, flashed her defiance. "I will never apologize to her. Never!"

"You will do as I say or you will go to your room and stay there!"

Helena turned to look at Regan with a venomous look. "You will never take my papa away from me," she cried. "I will not let you."

"Go to your room!" her father ordered.

Regan struggled to sit up, recognizing the possessiveness in Helena that she had felt for her own father. "Andreas," she said gently, for the moment intent only on comforting this young girl. "I don't think Helena means what she's saying. She's—"

"I mean it," Helena told her savagely. "I mean every word."

"I will give you five seconds to go to your room," her father repeated icily. "You understand?"

The fight went out of the young girl, her thin shoulders slumping. "Very well, papa," she said with youthful dignity. "But I will not apologize for speaking the truth." She left them, and seconds later they heard the slam of her bedroom door.

"Children can be the very devil," James Peters broke the silence. "I wouldn't worry; she's bound to come around."

"Yes," Andreas agreed grimly, his thoughts preoccupied. "I will see you out," he offered, the good manners bred into him coming to the fore.

"No need." James shut his bag with a snap of the lock. "Now, absolute rest for you for several days, young lady," he warned Regan.

A ghost of a smile softened Andreas's harsh features. "Do not worry, I intend to see that she stays in bed."

"I said she was to rest," came the doctor's humorous parting comment.

Regan was so angry she was shaking, hardly able to contain herself until the doctor had left the room. "How dare you discuss our having children with a complete stranger?" she demanded furiously.

"James is not a stranger. But you are, and I discussed them with you."

"You did not!"

"I told you I wanted sons," he said calmly. "It is only to be expected that there will be several daughters, too. The law of averages, I believe it is called."

"You heard Helena. She doesn't want me here."

His mouth tightened. "You will not be marrying Helena."

"She won't apologize, you know." The girl had as much arrogance and pride as her father, that much was already obvious.

"Then she will stay in her room."

"She can't stay there forever," Regan protested. "She's only young, Andreas. She's had you to herself a long time. She's bound to feel resentful."

He raised dark eyebrows. "You would defend her?"

She blushed at his surprise. "I can sympathize with her dislike of any other female in your life. Forget what she said to me. She's just hurt and upset. It will pass."

"It cannot be done," he said firmly. "I have never gone back on that sort of decision. I would lose her respect if I did so now."

"Not if you went and talked to her." Regan had no

idea why she was defending a girl who had shown her
nothing but dislike from the first.

"I will not talk to her," Andreas said distantly. "She
must come to you first and apologize."

He was implacable, she could see that. Poor Helena if
he was always this harsh with her. It was only natural
that the girl should react so strongly to a girl five years
her senior suddenly being introduced as her future stepmother, especially as the wedding was to take place
almost immediately after that meeting.

"Very well, Andreas." She made a show of accepting
his judgment, although in reality she had no intention of
doing any such thing. She would go and see Helena
herself and try to breach this rift she had with her
father, and she would go at the earliest opportunity.
Her chance came sooner than she had dared hope.

"I will be pleased if you agree that easily to all
of my instructions," Andreas told her with ill-concealed
arrogance. "For the moment you will wait here while
I go and change my shirt." He looked down ruefully
at the blood-stained material. "From the amount of
blood here I would have expected you to lose a limb at
least."

"And instead it's only a scratch!"

"No, Regan," he said seriously. "It is not a scratch. I
am well aware of the pain you are in."

"And you're glad about it!" she accused resentfully.

His hand on her chin wrenched her face around.
"No, I am not glad about it. I did not intend for you to
suffer physical pain."

Her eyes flashed. "Not even when you make love to
me?" she snapped.

His green eyes suddenly became almost black. "Especially not then," he said softly. "Pain is the last thing I
intend for you to feel at such a time. You are not averse
to my touching you now; then you will be even less so."

His meaning suddenly became clear. He intended to taunt her with her own reaction to him! "Did someone once tell you were a great lover?" she taunted to hide her sudden fear of him. Physically she could never deny him, she knew that. "I can think of no other reason you can have such an inflated opinion of your sexual prowess."

Andreas viewed her contemptuously. "You talk about sex in a way I do not think fitting for a woman."

She colored at his rebuke. "Evading the question, Andreas?" she mocked.

"Not at all," he drawled. "Do not worry, Regan. Soon, very soon, you will be able to judge for yourself. I will be five minutes changing my shirt, and then I will accompany you to the hospital."

"I'll be perfectly all right with the chauffeur; there's no need for you to come."

"You could not deny me one single minute of my fiancée's company?" he taunted. "I would be devastated."

"You don't trust me."

"I do not," he agreed harshly.

Left on her own Regan silently fumed at him. She had been hoping, foolishly, that the trip to the hospital would be her chance to escape. She should have known Andreas Vatis would never allow her such an opportunity.

She struggled to a sitting position, testing her foot on the floor, intending to hobble her way to Helena's room. The doctor had strapped her ankle up with a bandage, but nevertheless it hurt unbearably as she stood up. Still, she couldn't allow Helena's resentment time to fester and grow, not if she had to stay here for any length of time. The longer the time to the showdown between them, the higher the defenses the other girl would build up.

Helena's room was easily recognizable, as the sound

of the girl's sobbing was discernible through the closed
door. Regan knocked hard on that door.

"P-papa?" came the choked response.

Regan sighed, wishing she could say yes. "It's Regan,
Helena," she told her softly.

"Go away!" came the angry reply.

"I'm coming in, Helena," she said firmly. "Whether
you want me to or not."

"I do not—" Helena's protest broke off as Regan
entered the room. "I do not want you in here," she said
angrily, her green eyes glaring her dislike.

Goodness, this girl was going to be beautiful in a
year or two, when the curves had filled out to their full
promise of perfection, and when she had been persuaded to have the thick bushy dark hair tamed into some
sort of style. Andreas Vatis would have trouble keeping
the men away from his daughter in a couple of years'
time.

"I'm not surprised, Helena," she told the other girl
gently. "If I were you I would feel resentful, too."

The green eyes looked puzzled for a few brief seconds
and then dislike took over again. "You should not be
marrying my father," she snapped.

Regan frowned. It was a strange thing to say, not that
she didn't *want* her to marry Andreas, but that she
shouldn't. "Why?" she asked curiously.

"He should be married for love," Helena said
abruptly. "You do not love my father."

"How do you know that?"

Helena shrugged. "I have watched you with him, the
way you talk together. You do not love each other."

"And if we did?" Regan probed.

"Then I would be pleased." Her eyes hardened. "But
you do not love him, and I do not want you for his
wife."

"And if I told you I don't want to be his wife?"

Disbelief flashed briefly in those deep green eyes so

like Andreas's. "Why should you not want to marry him?" she asked indignantly.

"For the reason you've just stated. I don't love him."

Helena frowned. "Then why did you agree to marry him?"

"Because I—"

"Regan's reasons for becoming my wife need not concern you, Helena!" Andreas Vatis rasped from the open doorway.

Regan shot a nervous glance at his face dark with anger. He had a habit of appearing when she least expected or wanted to see him, his soft catlike tread making his approach indiscernible.

"But, papa, she—"

"Her name is Regan," Andreas said tautly. "You will call her by her given name," he ordered.

"Helena and I were just having a little chat," Regan cut in. "She's apologized for her rudeness earlier," she lied.

Green eyes pinpointed his daughter. "Is this true?"

Helena gave Regan a hesitant look, obviously undecided about angering her father again but reluctant to accept Regan's unasked-for help.

"Helena!"

The young girl's mouth set in a mutinous line. "No, it is not," she denied defiantly.

"That is what I thought." He flicked Regan an angry look. "You will not lie for my daughter again," he rasped.

No, she wouldn't. If Helena wasn't sensible enough to accept the hand of friendship when it was offered to her, then she would have to stay here in exile. After all, Regan didn't owe any member of this family any favors.

"I did not want her to, papa," Helena told him.

"I am pleased to hear it," he said curtly. "I am taking Regan to the hospital now. I will see you when I return, yes?"

Helena smiled tremulously. "Yes, please, papa."

The severity of his expression lightened. "You will join me for dinner," he instructed.

"Oh, yes, papa." Her face glowed.

Regan kept her anger bottled up inside as Andreas Vatis swung her up into his arms and carried her from the room. She chanced a brief look at him beneath lowered lashes as he walked down the stairs with no apparent exertion needed to carry her weight, noting the taut line of his mouth and his glacial eyes.

He helped her into the back seat of the Rolls-Royce before getting in beside her, curtly telling the chauffeur to drive on.

"I was only trying to be helpful," she eventually ventured.

He darted her an impatient look. "As you can see, neither Helena nor I appreciate that sort of help."

"But you were being so harsh on her," Regan protested.

"Helena respects authority," he told her tersely.

"But you said she would have to stay there, and I—"

"So she would have done," he cut in abruptly. "But not now. If she had aided you in your lie I would have found a suitable punishment for her. But Helena is not a deceitful child."

"Neither am I," Regan said angrily.

"You are not a child, I agree. But deceitful? Yes, I think you are that. But I will tell you now, Regan, that you are never again to try to involve my daughter in our differences."

"I wasn't—"

"Yes, you were," he contradicted grimly. "But it will not happen again."

"How can you be so sure?" she challenged.

"Because you are going to make me a dutiful wife," he informed her arrogantly. "And if you are that then you will also be a fitting mother for my daughter.''

"I'm not going to be your *dutiful* anything!'' Regan told him resentfully, her eyes sparkling with anger.

"You will be,'' he said calmly.

She gave him a suspicious look, not liking his attitude at all. ''What makes you so sure?''

"Because if there is one attempt on your part to disrupt my household, to alienate my daughter from me, or even to try to get away from here, I will make it public knowledge that you are the daughter of an attempted murderer.''

CHAPTER FOUR

THE WEDDING WAS A STRANGE AFFAIR, with the bride dressed in a pale blue suit, the only thing she had that was in the least suitable, her arm in a sling, her shoulder and ankle heavily bandaged, her face deathly pale. The latter was mainly through lack of sleep.

After Andreas Vatis's threat there had been no possibility of her getting any sleep last night. To think that he would make his allegations to anyone but her had shocked her immensely, and that he meant what he said was obvious. He wasn't a man who made idle threats, and she knew he meant every word of this one.

But she still couldn't believe what he said about her father. The man she remembered had been wild, fiery tempered, often impetuous, but he had not been a murderer. And one day she would prove that to this arrogant unforgiving man who was now her husband; she would make him sorry he had ever forced her into this marriage.

But for the moment she had to try to survive his verbal and physical abuse. Since that warning yesterday he had been chillingly polite, dealing with the doctors at the hospital as they had pronounced internal bruising to the ankle but no fracture. The drive back had been completed in cold silence, leaving her to the friendly solicitude of Mrs. Hall once they reached the house. And he had been a remote stranger as they were quietly married, after that spending several hours with Helena before disappearing into his study. How long that would last she had no idea. He had said he intended to torment her with this uncertainty, and the torment had already begun.

Helena had been subdued all day, although her father was excluded from this attitude. Regan had eaten her dinner in her room the evening before and so had no idea what had passed between father and daughter, but whatever it was they were obviously friends again.

The young girl disappeared outside somewhere when her father went to his study, and so Regan was left alone in the lounge feeling the outsider she was. She couldn't even get back to her bedroom on her own; the pain in her ankle was so severe she had to rely on Andreas to carry her from place to place.

Where on earth was everyone, she thought angrily. They had no right to leave her here alone, not today of all days. She rang angrily for Mrs. Hall.

"Yes, Mrs. Vatis?"

Regan didn't know whether to be angry or embarrassed by this form of address, finally resorting to the latter. "I—could you tell my husband I would like to see him, please?"

"Mr. Vatis is working in his study," the housekeeper told her uncertainly. "He doesn't usually like to be disturbed."

Regan gave her most endearing smile. "I'm sure he won't mind today, Mrs. Hall. He only went to make a couple of telephone calls," she invented. "Something must have happened to delay him."

"Well. . . .."

"Please, Mrs. Hall," she encouraged. "I'm sure it's just an oversight on his part."

The housekeeper smiled. "I'm sure it is. I'll just go and tell him."

Regan knew by the angry way Andreas entered the room a few minutes later that he hadn't been pleased by the interruption. His words confirmed this impression.

"What do you mean by sending my own housekeeper to summon me to your side?" he demanded furiously.

He had changed from the pale gray suit he had worn at the wedding that morning into a cream shirt and trousers, the lightness of his clothing emphasizing the natural darkness of his skin.

She smiled sweetly, pretending a calm she was far from feeling. He may want to dismiss her from his mind, but he had married her this morning and she wasn't going to make it easy for him to forget that, or that she had become his wife against her will. "I didn't *summon* you, Andreas," she said huskily. "I merely asked if you would come and see me."

"And now I have seen you," he said impatiently, "what do you want with me?"

"Unless it escaped your attention, we were married this morning," she reminded waspishly.

His gaze roved over her with insolent appraisal. "Are you asking me to perform my husbandly duties right now?" he drawled.

"Certainly not," Regan snapped. "All I'm asking for is a little consideration."

"I thought that by removing myself I was being considerate," Andreas taunted. "You have only to say if I was wrong."

"You weren't wrong." Her blue eyes flashed. "But won't your staff be a little surprised by your behavior? After all, you were the one who wanted to give this marriage the look of normality."

"That was before you took it into your head to fall out of a window."

"Oh, I didn't do that! I fell from a drainpipe—"

"After climbing out of a window," he reminded.

Did he have to remind her of her stupidity! But it wouldn't have been stupid if she had just managed to climb that last few feet to the ground undetected. She

would have been free by now, far away from here and
Andreas Vatis.

"You forced me into it." She glared at him.

"Perhaps. But all it brought you was the pain you are
now suffering. It is still painful, is it not?"

"Yes!"

He shook his head. "It was a stupid thing to do." He
repeated his words of the day before.

"I was frightened at the time!"

"You mean you are not still?"

Regan hated his mockery. But she couldn't refute his
words; she was frightened, very frightened. Andreas
Vatis caused that fear, with his hard savage face and
harsh vengeful manner.

"I can see you are." His mouth twisted. "So perhaps
you have changed your mind about wanting to see me?"

"No, I haven't," she retorted, stung by the contempt
he made no effort to hide. "You can take your afternoon tea with me. I've asked Mrs. Hall to bring it in."

Andreas stiffened, the firm angles of his face darken-
ing with anger. "You would dare to issue orders to me?"

Regan wasn't deceived by the softness of his tone. But
she wouldn't be daunted by him. She wouldn't be!
"Stop being so. . .so Greek," she said crossly.

He frowned. "But I am a Greek. How can I be other
than what I am?"

"You don't have to be so damned arrogant all the
time. What's wrong with taking your afternoon tea with
me?"

"I do not like being ordered to do anything. And I do
not take afternoon tea. I rarely have time for it."

"Not even on your wedding day?"

He raised his eyebrows. "Today is no different to any
other day. I have work to do. I leave early in the morning."

"Leave?" she echoed sharply. "You're going away?"

"Only to London, as I usually do."

Regan frowned. "You do?"

"But of course." He broke off as Mrs. Hall wheeled
in the tea things, then nodded his dismissal of her. "You
did not think I worked from here, did you?" he asked
Regan.

She had to admit she had thought that, although
Cornwall seemed a strange place to run his empire from.
"How often do you go to London?"

"I usually leave early Monday morning and return
late Friday evening."

"And will I be going with you?"

"You?" He looked surprised. "Why should I take
you with me?"

Color flooded her cheeks. "I just thought—"

He gave a harsh laugh. "Three nights a week in the
same bed will be enough," he told her mockingly.
"Although if you please me I may take you with me at
some later date."

Regan had no intention of pleasing him. With his
dominating presence removed she felt her chances of
getting away from here increasing. He could hardly
order his staff to keep watch over her. "Why do you
choose to leave Helena here when you're away in London so often?"

"I do not stay in London, I only make that my base. I
travel all over the world, and the life of travel is not for
a young girl. I do not think London a suitable place to
leave a girl of Helena's temperament in the charge of
servants."

"I don't suppose Helena considers herself young at
nearly sixteen."

"Perhaps not," Andreas accepted dryly. "And she
probably is not. It is only another year until she is to
marry."

Regan gasped. "How do you know that?"

"She has been promised to Dmitri Papalos since she
was two years old," he informed her distantly.

"And how old is he?"

"He is nineteen now."

"And are they in love?"

"Love!" he scorned. "They have not met since they were children, so I would doubt that very much."

After the disaster of his first marriage Regan could understand Andreas not marrying for love a second time, but she couldn't understand him subjecting Helena to an arranged marriage. Her disgust must have shown, because Andreas again looked angry.

"Do not interfere in things you do not understand," he told her harshly.

"Oh, I understand; I understand only too well. But Helena doesn't appear to me to be the sort of girl to accept having her life organized for her."

"She will do as I say," Andreas said haughtily.

Regan couldn't see many people wanting to disagree with this man. There was a slumbering savagery about him that dared anyone to defy him, a promise of fierce retribution if crossed. Hadn't her father recognized this in him? Hadn't he guessed that Andreas Vatis would not treat the stealing of his wife lightly? Or had her father just not cared? He had always been wild, that wild streak widely reported in the newspapers. Or perhaps Andreas hadn't possessed this cruel anger eleven years ago. This seemed the more reasonable explanation.

"Do you enjoy playing God?" she now scorned.

"God?" he taunted, a humorless smile to his lips. "I thought you envisaged me as the devil?"

"I do!" she told him heatedly. "But it's playing God choosing the boy for Helena to marry. Goodness, they could hate each other."

His eyes were narrowed and bitter. "And you think that marrying for love would make her any happier?" He moved to stare out of the window, his broad shoulders rigid, not an atom of gentleness in his whole body.

"I married Gina for love," he continued grimly. "By the time she left me I was almost relieved to see her go."

"Then why—"

"Which is not to say," he cut in firmly, "that I did not still consider it a deep insult when your father took her away from me."

"But if you were going to separate anyway?"

"We were not," Andreas said stiffly. "A Greek marriage is forever."

"Is that why you only married me in a registry office? So that you can get rid of me easily later on?" she challenged.

He nodded. "Perhaps." He frowned. "Your red hair...?"

"Yes?" She was surprised by the sudden change of subject.

"You get this from your mother?"

"Would that make it more acceptable?" she flashed.

He raised his eyebrows. "To me, you mean?"

"Of course!"

"I am becoming used to your auburn tresses," he dismissed carelessly.

"I hope that doesn't mean you're becoming attracted to me?" she said worriedly.

"Whether I am or I am not is immaterial—"

"Because you intend making love to me anyway?"

"Exactly," he agreed haughtily.

"In that case I hope you don't mind the fact that my hair color comes from my father. Have you forgotten the reddish tint to his brown hair?"

His face had once again hardened to grim anger. "I have forgotten nothing about your father. Nothing!"

She could see he hadn't by the glitter of hatred in his brilliant green eyes. "I still think you're wrong about him. I'm sure he couldn't deliberately have tried to hurt anyone."

"If you believe this then why did you marry me?"

"Because I'm going to enjoy watching your face when I prove to you how wrong you are about him. I'll enjoy watching you grovel," she added.

Andreas stiffened. "I grovel to no man...or woman. Especially a woman." He walked out of the room, his back rigid.

He *would* grovel, she would make sure of that! If only she could think of some way to prove her father's innocence.

BY THE TIME REGAN HAD MANAGED TO HOBBLE downstairs the next day, Andreas had long gone—thank goodness. And Helena was in with her tutor, a rather shy young man who lived in one of the estate cottages.

She met Tom Stills at lunchtime, a rather less formal meal than any she had so far taken in this house, probably because of the removal of Andreas's presence. Tom Stills proved to be a man in his early twenties, rather handsome in an unassuming sort of way, with hair the color of her own, although maybe not quite so red, with dark velvety brown eyes, and a lithe athletic figure. His brown checked sports coat and plain brown trousers were serviceable as well as smart.

He had been employed as Helena's private tutor for the last six months, and could obviously hardly believe his luck, as the undemanding job also provided him with accommodation that was completely private.

"Andreas tells me you're preparing Helena for her exams." Regan opened the conversation, well aware that her new stepdaughter's glaring dislike at her across the small dining table was not conducive to her starting a conversation with her.

"Yes, I am," Tom agreed eagerly.

"And how is she doing?"

"Very well." He nodded enthusiastically.

"Don't you find it boring teaching just one pupil?" Regan asked curiously.

He flushed slightly. "Well, I—"

"Are you implying that Tom—Mr. Stills should be bored with *me*?" Helena burst out indignantly.

That was exactly what Regan had meant to imply, hoping to draw Helena into the conversation. . . and she had succeeded. And how she had succeeded! The young girl was furious at her inference. Regan deliberately gave her a calmly innocent look. "Don't you think he should be?"

"No, I do not! And you have no right to ask him questions about my progress. My father may have married you, but you did not even manage to hold him for two days. That proves what sort of wife you are."

Tom Stills looked uncomfortable. "Helena!" he said sternly. "I don't think you should be talking to, er, your stepmother in that way."

"She is not—"

"The question is, Helena," Regan cut in, "not what sort of wife I am, but what sort of husband your father is. And he is obviously the type of husband thoughtful enough not to expect too much from a wife who is in great pain." If only he were that thoughtful!

The young girl flushed at her meaning. "My papa did not share your bed last night!"

"Helena—"

"It's perfectly all right, Mr. Stills," Regan assured him. "Helena can say what she likes to me. I can take it." She could take anything from the daughter after listening to the insults of the father.

Helena glared at her. "You have no right to question anyone about me—"

"I was merely wondering—"

"Do not *wonder* anything," Helena interrupted rudely. "If my father wished you to know anything, then he would have told you."

"He can hardly do that when he isn't here."

"Then you will have to wait until he returns." Helena

stood up. "I am ready to resume my studies, Mr. Stills."

"Run along to the schoolroom," Regan ordered. "I wish to talk to your tutor "

"I will not 'run along' anywhere!" Helena predictably exploded. "I—"

"Do as your stepmother says," Tom Stills told her quietly.

"But—"

"Helena!" His soft voice carried a wealth of authority.

"Very well," she agreed reluctantly, giving one last resentful glare at Regan.

Regan sighed once she was alone with Tom Stills. "I'm sorry about that. Antagonizing her seems to be the only way I get a response." Actually she was surprised that the young girl had done as this man told her; it seemed to be completely out of character.

"I've always found her very cooperative," he said stiffly.

Regan thought he seemed rather indignant on his pupil's behalf. Surely he couldn't have more than a scholarly interest in his pupil? The idea seemed incredible and she dismissed it immediately. He probably just resented her unexpected appearance here, as Helena did.

"I hope you'll bear with me, Mr. Stills," she said almost shyly. "I think I could be a good friend to Helena if she would let me." After all, that had been her first intention when she came here.

"Helena doesn't give her friendship easily."

"She's given it to you."

Color entered his cheeks. "I hope so. It would be difficult teaching someone who disliked me," he added hastily.

"I'm sure," Regan agreed slowly. "Thank you for talking to me," she smiled at him.

He frowned. "But we haven't discussed anything."

"It's enough for me to know Helena has a friend in you."

She mused over that friendship as she sat alone in the lounge drinking her coffee. The idea of something deeper than friendship between tutor and pupil no longer seemed so incredible. The two of them were alone here during the week, giving them ample time to become more than fond of each other. No doubt Andreas would scoff at the idea, claiming that Helena was no more than a child. But Regan knew very well that nowadays girls of sixteen were already adults, with adult feelings.

She watched Helena and Tom Stills closely over the next few days—with her ankle and shoulder out of action she had little else to do—and although Helena seemed more than a little interested in her tutor, Regan had to compliment him on the way he treated her with casual friendliness.

By Friday afternoon Regan was completely bored with her own company. Besides the luncheons she shared with Helena and Tom Stills, she had spent the rest of the time pretty much on her own, and consequently was no nearer getting to know her stepdaughter. Her shoulder and ankle were well on the way to healing; the doctor had removed the dressing from her shoulder altogether. Despite the purple and black bruising she was now able to move it without too much pain, which was why on Friday afternoon she decided to take a swim in the pool at the back of the house.

She had lost weight this past week, and her pale green bikini was almost too big for her. She swam languorously up and down the pool, dreading Andreas's return that evening. He had telephoned Helena one evening, asking to speak to Regan. His inquiries about her health had been made out of politeness and not genuine concern, and she had made sure their conversation was kept to a minimum. And tonight he would be returning, and who knows what their relationship would be when he returned to London on Monday morning. He was right—the not knowing when he would claim her for his wife was worse than anything else in the whole of this sham of a marriage.

That there would be no tenderness and understanding in their union as husband and wife she had no doubt, and just the thought of Andreas Vatis claiming her body for his own made her break out in a cold sweat. How could he, how could any man, make love to a woman as cold-bloodedly as he proposed doing? He said he had no desire for her, had proved as much by his cold indifference as he had caressed her so that she was at fever pitch, and so his promise to make her his wife made her feel nauseous.

She jumped nervously as someone glided into the water beside her. Surely Andreas hadn't returned early! She almost sighed her relief as Helena surfaced a few feet away, the black bathing suit she wore of suitable respectability for a young girl.

She ignored Regan completely, swimming up and down the pool with studied ease, her long dark hair flattened down her back, her slender arms moving slowly in and out of the water.

After the first few minutes Regan shruggingly got out onto the side of the pool, getting onto a lounger and rubbing suntan oil on her arms and shoulders. She would just sit here and wait; after all, Helena had to get out sometime. She had quite a long wait, as the girl seemed to be in no hurry to leave the warm water.

Regan watched as the girl toweled her body dry a few feet away from her, wondering if Andreas had taken a good look at his daughter lately, seen the mature curves that weren't noticeable under the baggy blouses and skirts she usually wore.

"Why do you stare at me?" Helena suddenly challenged.

"Do I?"

"You know you do," Helena accused. "All the time you stare at me."

Regan stood up, pulling on the thin cotton robe that matched the color of her bikini. "I'm sure you're imagining it."

"You know I am not," the other girl said vehemently. "And your behavior toward Tom—Mr. Stills is disgusting."

"Disgusting?" she repeated slowly. "What's disgusting about it?"

"Everything! You constantly vie for his attention during lunch, talk to him on subjects I cannot converse in, discuss—"

"I'm sure you're exaggerating, Helena," she disputed lightly. "Name one subject we've discussed that you couldn't join in."

"Going to college!" Helena pulled on her own toweling robe. "It is unfair of you to talk of it when you know I have no experience of it."

"I don't think I was the one to bring the subject up."

"Tom was only being polite," Helena snapped.

So she was right—Helena did think of her tutor as Tom! "Then you should feel pleased that he has manners enough to want me to join in the conversation."

"Join in!" the young girl derided angrily. "You try to dominate it. Before you came Mr. Stills needed no company but my own. Now you are trying to take him away from me, trying to make him attracted to you."

"You're being ridiculous," Regan dismissed. "I find Mr. Stills interesting to talk to." If only because he was the only person here who treated her as a normal human being. "And I would hardly try to make him attracted to me when I'm married to your father." Although it might be worth it just to see Andreas's anger when he realized what she had done. But she couldn't do that to Tom Stills, knowing that Andreas would surely sack him.

"I do not yet know the reason he married you, but I do know it was not through any love on his part."

Regan assumed a mocking expression. "Have you never heard of lust, Helena?" she taunted.

Color flooded the young girl's cheeks. "My father does not *lust* after you, either," she scorned.

"Can you be sure about that?"

"Of course I can. You have little to attract him." Her look was insulting.

Regan shook her head, a smile playing across her lips. "A moment ago you were accusing me of trying to attract Tom Stills... and succeeding. You can't have it both ways, Helena; either I am attractive or I'm not."

Her cool manner obviously angered the younger girl. "You are not!"

"Then—"

"Ah, Helena, Regan," remarked a deep familiar accented voice. "I'm pleased to see the two of you have become friends in my absence."

Regan looked blushingly at her husband. The cream suit and dark brown shirt he wore made his dark skin appear even swarthier. He looked tired, with lines of weariness beside his nose and mouth and a certain dullness to his usually bright eyes. Just looking at him made her nervous. If only her ankle and shoulder hadn't made it impossible for her to go anywhere this last week! But next week, next week she would escape from here, would find out the truth about her father. She only hoped Andreas had no plans to make her his wife before she was able to do that.

"Papa!" Helena ran over to him, throwing her arms about his neck to receive his hug. "I am so pleased you are home," she told him tremulously.

He tilted her chin. "Your enthusiasm pleases me," he said gently. "But you are not usually so excited by my return," he frowned.

"It is not excitement, papa, it is relief."

His frown darkened. "Relief?"

"Yes, papa," she nodded slowly. "I am sorry to tell you this, but it is not *my* friendship your wife has been cultivating these last four days."

Andreas looked at Regan over his daughter's shoulders, his gaze razor sharp. "Explain, Helena," he ordered.

"I do not think I should. Besides, I am getting cold." She shivered as if to prove her point. "I must go in and dress." With a triumphant glance at Regan she entered the house.

Andreas walked slowly over to where Regan still reclined on the lounger, standing darkly over her. "In my daughter's absence," he said curtly, "you will explain her remarks."

No hello or inquiry after her health, just a demand for an explanation to an implication of his daughter's. "Innuendos, don't you mean?" Regan retorted sharply.

He put a weary hand to the temple with the thin scar disappearing into the hairline. "Remarks, innuendos, what does it matter? Surely I am entitled to an answer?"

"Then go and get one from your daughter," she told him abruptly, her voice cold.

His fingers bit painfully into her uninjured arm, and he came down on his haunches beside her. "You have become no more amenable in my absence. I like that," he smiled. "I like that very much."

Regan was very pale. "Get your hands off me!" she ordered through gritted teeth.

"Gladly." He instantly stood up. "Whose friendship would you seek here? Am I right in thinking you have not left the house?"

"How could I with an injured ankle?" But she would, she would!

"Or you would no longer be here, hmm?" He guessed her unspoken words. "We shall have to see what we can do about your desire to leave. Perhaps try to change your mind," he added softly.

"Never!" she said vehemently.

"We shall see," he told her calmly. "For now I will go and talk to Helena. It appears that I must get my answers from her."

Regan turned away, refusing to even look at him. God knows what tale Helena would tell him. But what did she care. Andreas Vatis's approval was the last thing she needed. . . or wanted.

Once he had left her she went up to her own room to shower and dress before dinner. Andreas had returned earlier than expected. She hoped tonight wasn't to be the night he had decided to come through the door that connected their bedrooms. She would rather die.

Happen it did, and right at that moment, the door hitting the opposite wall with a crash. It didn't need two guesses to know the reason for his anger. Helena had obviously embroidered on the subject of this proposed friendship between Regan and Tom Stills.

She stood up, pulling her silky wrap farther around her naked body, indignant at this intrusion into her privacy. "What do you want?" she asked rudely.

"Certainly not what you seem to have no compunction in offering this last week to a man in my employ," he snapped furiously, his eyes gleaming like coals. "This is what you have been offering to him, is it not?" He flicked open the lapel of her wrap contemptuously.

"Don't be obscene! Tom Stills—"

"Yes? Tom Stills what?" he demanded to know. "At least it appears that you and Helena have the same man in mind." His eyes narrowed even more.

Regan looked up from hastily re-covering the creamy expanse of breast he had revealed. "There are no other men here," she reminded scathingly.

He began to pace up and down the room, still in the cream suit and brown shirt, the lines of strain deepened.

"I suppose that is your excuse for throwing yourself at a complete stranger?"

Helena *had* been at work! "I haven't thrown myself at anyone, a stranger or otherwise. I've had a few polite conversations with the man, that's all. I'm sure that if you asked him he would confirm what I'm telling you."

His mouth twisted. "I am sure he would," he taunted. "You probably have him so infatuated he would agree to anything. But I did not have you watched and guarded all these years so that you could be unfaithful with another man *during* our marriage, and especially not before *I* have become your lover. Tom Stills will leave my employ at once," he told her coldly.

Regan frowned. "Isn't that a little drastic?"

If anything his expression darkened even further—if that were possible! "Your defense of the man only confirms his guilt. . . and yours."

She shrugged. "I wasn't thinking of myself."

His mouth set in a grim line. "Of him, then."

"Not of him, either," Regan interrupted in a bored voice, watching below lowered lashes as his interest quickened.

Andreas gave her a suspicious look, his pacing coming to an end. "Then of whom?"

"Why, of Helena, of course," she looked at him with wide innocent blue eyes. "How long do you suppose she's been in love with her tutor?" she queried calmly.

CHAPTER FIVE

AN ANGRY FLUSH colored Andreas's hard cheeks. "Are you insane?" he exploded.

"Not at all." She wasn't daunted by his anger.

"How dare you stand there and say my daughter is in love with her tutor!"

She began brushing her newly washed silky hair, watching in the mirror as it bounced back into its wavy style. "Don't be such a snob, Andreas. After all, you married a companion. Helena is only following your example and falling for one of the lower classes."

He snatched the hairbrush out of her hand and threw it on the floor. "I married a waspish, mischief-making young woman! And I was not being snobbish; I was merely showing amazement for your assumption that Helena is old enough to feel any kind of emotion for the opposite sex."

"Oh, she feels them." Regan bent to pick up the brush, feeling it safer to replace it on the dressing table rather than resume brushing her hair and further evoke Andreas's anger. "She's almost sixteen, Andreas. And you told me yourself that she's getting married in a year's time."

"But not to Tom Stills!"

"I've already warned you that Helena is not the sort of person to have her life organized for her. Watching her this week, talking to her, I've come to realize that's even more true than I first thought. Helena will marry whom she chooses. Not the man you pick for her."

"Her husband is already decided; she has always known this."

Regan shook her head. "Knowing and accepting are two different things. One day you could just wake up and find that she's run off with Tom Stills."

"Are you telling me that he has been *encouraging* this infatuation?" His voice was dangerously soft.

"No. What I am saying is that he's attracted to her enough to agree to it if she pressures him enough." She had sat back and watched as the pupil maneuvered the teacher this last week, had watched as Tom Stills became more and more emotionally involved with the young girl who had made no secret of her attraction to him. Of course, all young girls became infatuated with one of their teachers at some time during their schooling, but the fact that there was only one pupil made it a much more dangerous situation. After all, Tom Stills was only a man, and like any other he was flattered by female adoration.

"Then he will leave at once," Andreas announced autocratically.

"I don't think that would be a good idea."

He looked at her with those suspiciously piercing eyes, making it all the more difficult for her to believe he had sight in only one of them. "Why would it not?"

"Because I'm very much afraid Helena would just follow him."

"She is underage. I would bring her back; the law says I have the right."

"She'll be sixteen next month, old enough, many people would say, to make her own decision about her life's partner. Especially as she and the man you have chosen for her haven't met for a number of years."

"I do not believe you," he snapped. "You want me to keep him here for your sake. This story of he and Helena is pure fabrication, a lie so that your lover can stay here and you may continue your affair with him."

Regan sighed. "All I'm suggesting is that you perhaps invite Dmitri Papalos over here for a few weeks. Put Helena in contact with a boy of her own age."

Andreas looked at her suspiciously. "Why should you care that my daughter may run off with a completely unsuitable man?"

"I don't care for your sake; I hate you," she told him calmly, meeting the livid anger in his eyes with an unblinking stare. "But I've grown fond of Helena, despite her obvious dislike of me, and I would hate to see her ruin her life."

"You are sure this suggestion that I bring Dmitri here is not being made so that you can have yet another man to flirt with?"

Her eyes flashed her hatred of him. "Did I at any time during your surveillance of me these last years give you the impression that I'm a flirt?" she demanded tautly.

He shrugged his broad shoulders. "Probably not. But you could be doing this to thwart me."

She gave him a scathing look. "I don't feel enough toward you to give you the time of day if you asked me for it, so I have no intention of becoming a flirt just to get at you."

Anger made his face a cruel mask. "You will apologize for that remark," he ordered curtly. "Now!"

"I'm not a sixteen-year-old that you can browbeat and push around in that arrogant way of yours," she retorted angrily. "I won't apologize for speaking the truth...and you can't make me!"

"Are you sure of that?" he asked softly.

"Well, you can hardly send me to my room as you did Helena. I'm already in it," she told him tauntingly.

"In that you are wrong. This is not your room, but *our* room. The room next to this is only a dressing room, with a single bed for my use when you are indisposed. But you are not indisposed now, are you?" He took a threatening step toward her. "And I could do with a rest on that comfortable bed before dinner. I returned from a fleeting visit to Athens this morning, and I worked on my papers during the drive down here."

Regan backed away. No wonder she had such a huge double bed; this was the master bedroom! "Go ahead and rest," she invited nervously. "I'll try not to disturb you when I leave."

"But I am already disturbed." He stood between her and the sanctuary of the bathroom, deliberately so, she thought. "And I have no intention of letting you leave."

"Look, I'm sorry for what I said." Her eyes were huge and very blue in her sudden fear. "I...I didn't mean to be rude," she added desperately as he took another stealthy step toward her. God, she couldn't back much farther, only another couple of feet and she would have her back to the wall...literally! "Please, Andreas." She hated herself for pleading with this monster of a man, a man who could take a wife just for revenge, but what other choice did she have? He looked very determined. "I, er, I want to get dressed."

"Later," he dismissed huskily. "Later we will both get dressed. But for now you will *un*dress me." He stood in front of her as she pressed against the wall.

Regan looked at him with the frightened eyes of a doe cornered by a rampant stag. "I've apologized." She was begging now. "Please let me go."

He shook his head, a smile of satisfaction on his face. "Your apology came too late, Regan," he said softly, putting up a hand to touch the soft auburn waves of her hair. "I have thought of this the last few days," he surprised her by admitting. "I do not find it so unattractive, after all. In fact, I have been wondering if your fire is all on the outside."

In this mood of seduction Andreas was mesmerizing,

and Regan could once more feel herself weakening to the experienced touch of his hands. What was it about this man's caresses that so aroused her, the trembling of her body letting him know exactly what effect he was having on her?

His thumbs probed the hollows beneath her earlobes, his hands holding her head immobile as his dark head swooped to claim her mouth in a nerve-shattering kiss. His tongue probed her clamped lips, its sensuous tip a drugging caress, her lips parting of their own volition as he deepened the kiss to intimacy.

His body lowered against her shorter height, and the hardness of his thighs transferred his desire for her. "Is this to be a fight?" he murmured throatily against her earlobe. "Or will you make it easy for me?"

Maybe if he hadn't spoken he would have found it all *too* easy to seduce her into bed with him. But he had spoken, and the sound of his voice was like a splash of cold water to her heightened senses. She began to struggle against him, but was unable to move him even one inch away from her.

Andreas looked down at her with a demonically triumphant face. "I had hoped it would be a fight," he told her with satisfaction.

Regan cringed with shame as he bent her back over his arm, carrying her to the bed before pushing aside her silky wrap, bending his head and taking one rosy nipple between his lips. The pleasure that shot through Regan's body at the caress of his tongue was like nothing she had ever experienced before—every inch of her seemed to be alive only to his touch.

That Andreas was enjoying her unwilling pleasure was evident as he raised his head, a deep satisfaction in his dark features. His hand moved to take over the caressing of his mouth as he moved up her body to probe her throat with his lips.

Tears of humiliation and shame cascaded down

Regan's cheeks at her helplessness, his body on hers seeming already to possess her. She lay almost naked beneath him, her wrap completely pushed aside, only the silk shirt and trousers he wore a barrier against his complete domination of her body.

"I shall hate you afterward," she found the strength to whisper, even while her legs entangled with his and she strained him closer to her.

He gave a throaty laugh, not even bothering to raise his head. "You hate me now, and you can only hate once."

"If you take me now I'll never let you near me again!"

Again he laughed. "I shall take you any time I want," he announced arrogantly. "I have to do this—" his thumb caressed her breast "—and you will accept this." He savagely parted her lips, his tongue moving to deepen the kiss.

It was only the sound of someone knocking on the door several minutes later that made him stop. For Regan it was a welcome interruption, but the dark anger on Andreas's face showed he did not feel the same way.

"Mrs. Vatis?" came the housekeeper's voice.

"I'll have to answer, Andreas," Regan told him in a whisper. "She knows I'm in here, and she'll think I'm ill if I don't open the door."

With a deep angry sigh he rolled away from her. "Answer then," he snapped coldly.

She pulled her wrap around her before moving to answer the door. "Yes, Mrs. Hall?" she said breathlessly. "I'm sorry I was so long answering. I—I just came from the shower." She hoped the shaking of her limbs wasn't obvious to this woman, but she was still very much in the clutches of the sexual excitement Andreas had aroused.

"I was just wondering if you knew where Mr. Vatis is," Mrs. Hall explained. "You see, there's an important telephone call from Athens, and I—"

"I am here, Mrs. Hall." Andreas opened the door wider to reveal himself as he slowly buttoned up his shirt. "The call is from Athens, you say?"

The housekeeper looked blushingly from one to the other of them. "I'm sorry, I—I didn't realize—"

"It is not important," he dismissed, moving out into the corridor, taking hold of the housekeeper's elbow and walking way. "Did the person of this so important telephone call give a name?"

"It's a lady, sir. But I didn't think to ask for a name."

Regan didn't wait to hear anymore, slamming the door to her bedroom. It would be one of Andreas's women friends, the reason for his fleeting visit to Athens this week, no doubt. Perhaps the poor woman couldn't do without him even for one day.

The thought of Andreas leaving some other woman's arms this morning was sickening to her, especially as without Mrs. Hall's timely interruption he would have had no compunction about making love to *her* this afternoon. His intention of making her his wife when he had just left another woman was typical of his behavior toward her—insulting and degrading.

She didn't know if he intended returning to her bedroom after he had taken the call, but if he did he would find her dressed and calm, and not the quivering woman he had just left. She had to avoid being alone with him in future; she simply couldn't fight him. She was falling more and more into the sexual trap he intended setting for her, and there wasn't a thing she could do about it.

She was studiously painting her fingernails when Andreas walked back into the bedroom. She didn't like the easy familiarity with which he did it, but she could hardly object, not when he had just informed her it was his bedroom, too.

"I have to return to Athens immediately," he told her without preamble, going through the connecting doorway to the dressing room to collect a few clothes.

Regan burned with anger. "Is she that good?" she snapped, giving up on her nails as she made a mess of yet another one.

Andreas appeared in the open doorway, a dark frown to his features. "Who are you talking about?"

"Your friend," she sneered.

"Marisa?" He gave a mocking smile. "Yes, I suppose you could say she is good—very good, in fact," he added with relish.

"Thank God she'll be the one to share your bed tonight," Regan spat the words at him.

"For tonight she may have that privilege; tomorrow I will come back to you," he told her haughtily.

"B-back to me?" she queried nervously, watching the precision with which he packed the clothes necessary for his overnight stay, an ability no doubt gained through his years of constant travel.

He shut the case with a snap of the lock. "Yes, dear wife," he taunted with cruel humor. "I have decided that when I return I will be sharing this room with you. You will like that."

It sounded like an order. "Will I?"

He nodded. "At least then you will not have the uncertainty of not knowing when I will demand to be your husband. Besides, my appetite for you has been aroused. By this time next year I expect you to have presented me with my first son."

"Even though according to you his grandfather was an attempted murderer?"

"He may have done that, but he was not insane," Andreas said coldly. "On the contrary, he was very intelligent. But where women were concerned he had a weak spot. Your mother must have had a terrible life with him."

"Are you saying there were women even before my mother died?" Regan was white with disbelief.

"There have always been women. Your father rarely

took your mother abroad with him, preferring to have his freedom to enjoy the females who invariably appeared at the racing track intent on sleeping with one of the drivers. Your father never disappointed them.''

"I'm sure you've taken your share," she sneered.

He regarded her with icy disdain. "They amount to little more than prostitutes, giving their bodies for a meal and bed for the night.''

"You didn't answer my question.''

"I was not aware it had been one.''

"Well, I'm asking it now. How many of those women have you had?''

"After my marriage failed I took advantage of a few of these girls, before I realized they disgusted me.''

"And during your marriage?''

"None at all.''

"Didn't you have your 'friends'?'' Regan scorned.

"No. And if you had ever met Gina you would know why.''

Regan blushed fiery red. "I see," she said stiffly.

"No, you do not," he gave a bitter smile. "My wife was an American; she had no compunction about causing a scene if she thought I had been unfaithful to her.''

"And how do you know I won't do the same?'' she challenged.

"Because if you did I would put you over my knee and spank you.''

"Don't worry—who you sleep with doesn't bother me.''

He raised dark eyebrows. "Not even if it is yourself?''

She visibly flinched. Of course it bothered her if he shared her bed—it destroyed all her girlish illusions of love and marriage.

"I can see by your expression that it does. Never mind, Regan, you will soon know what it is like to be in a man's arms.'' He unbuttoned his dark shirt, pulling a fresh one out of the wardrobe. "Try to make friends with Helena while I am gone. As you have already found out, she makes almost as formidable an adversary as I do."

"And what of Tom Stills?"

Andreas's face darkened. "For the moment he can stay; he is needed for the next few weeks at least for Helena's examinations. But if I once think he is attracted to you he will leave immediately. I will not have a second wife who has the morals of an alley cat."

"Your wife was unfaithful?"

He frowned. "Not until your father came along. Greek wives are not unfaithful."

"I will be, if I get the chance," she cried vehemently.

"This you will not have," he told her coldly. "In a few days we will be going to Vatis, my Greek island."

"*Your* island?" She didn't really know why she was surprised; he must be rich enough to own the whole of Greece, let alone one island. And obviously it belonged to him—it was named after him. "You go there a lot?" she asked, a more relevant question.

He shrugged, taking off one shirt and replacing it with the fresh one, giving Regan a leisurely look at his tanned, muscled torso, with not an ounce of excess flesh on his body. "Whenever I get the chance, which is not very often. I spend maybe two months of the year there, completely cut off from what we call civilization."

"You mean it has no amenities?" she gasped.

He smiled at her shock. "No, I do not mean that. I have houses in all the capitals of Europe, an apartment in the States, and I can run the company as well from one as I can from any other. They are all fully equipped and my staff flies with me. But on Vatis there is only peace and relaxation. No staff, except to run the household, no unexpected guests, and most important of all, no telephones."

"Then I'm surprised you didn't take me straight

there. I could hardly have caused trouble somewhere like that.''

"You will not cause trouble here," he informed her arrogantly. "I have only to accuse your father to bring you back in line.''

Except for one little thing, something she had thought of in his absence. If he accused her father he would be openly admitting to marrying the daughter of a man who had tried to kill him. She didn't think he would want the publicity involved any more than she did. In fact, she was counting on that being the case.

Andreas's eyes narrowed. "What are you thinking?"

"I was just wondering how anyone reached you on the island if there was an emergency.'' She hastily thought of something to say.

He seemed satisfied with her answer. "Planning your escape already?" he taunted.

"And if I were?"

"You would not get very far. I have men patroling the shoreline in boats. Vatis is the one place I will allow no one who is not specifically invited. The radio in the main house can only be used with my own personal code.''

"And only you know it,'' she guessed resignedly, seeing herself incarcerated in the middle of the Aegean Sea, with no one within miles to help her.

"Exactly,'' he agreed with a smile, pulling on the cream jacket that matched his trousers. "We will begin making the arrangements for our departure when I return.''

"*Our* departure?"

"Helena will be coming with us. A short holiday before her examinations will do her no harm. Tom Stills will remain in England,'' he added harshly.

"I told you I don't give a damn about him.''

"It appears you do not give a damn about anyone,'' Andreas snapped. "It is time someone changed that.''

"I care about what you're doing to me," she cried. "I care about the way you talk to me, the way you treat me. I care about those things."

"If you are trying to appeal to my better nature I think I should tell you I do not have one. That was destroyed as surely as the sight in this eye was destroyed." His fingers touched the thin white scar barely discernible above his left eye.

"Is there nothing that can be done about that? They can do such wonderful things now, and—"

"Nothing can be done," he said coldly. "The nerves were too badly damaged. Do not worry, Regan, it makes me no less a man."

Nothing could do that. Andreas Vatis was too essentially male to ever be anything else. Just a brief glimpse of his naked torso seconds earlier had been enough to rekindle the passion he had aroused a short time ago. And the fact that she felt this way disgusted her. The only trouble was, when Andreas came near her she couldn't think clearly.

"I will show you." He pulled her roughly into his arms and kissed her hard on the mouth. "Take care, Regan. When I return tomorrow we will make this marriage a real one."

Except that she didn't intend being here when he got back; she intended being long gone. And she would prove to him how wrong he had been about the past. "Have fun with Marisa." She pushed away from him, relieved when he made no effort to hold on to her. "But I'm sure you'll do that, anyway."

"I am sure I will, too. Until tomorrow, my obedient little wife." He picked up the small suitcase and left. She could hear him talking to someone outside and then silence.

Regan wandered back into the bedroom, coming up short as she saw Helena standing in the open doorway, a curiously still Helena, with glittering green eyes.

Suddenly she sprang into life, coming furiously into the room. "So you are *his* daughter," she hissed. "The daughter of James Matthews."

Regan's eyes widened. "You were listening?"

"Of course. How else would I know the truth about you? My father's reason for marrying you now becomes obvious." She looked at Regan with distaste. "Your father took my mother away."

"There are always two sides to every story, Helena. My father—"

"Was a cheap womanizer with a smooth line of chatter that no woman could resist, be she single or married."

The words were strangely adult, too adult for the fiery Helena, which left only one other person who could have said them—Andreas Vatis. "That's a biased opinion," Regan dismissed angrily, "made by a bitter man."

"My father was not bitter," Helena denied heatedly. "He was more disgusted than bitter by my mother's infidelity with such a man."

"Oh, I suppose if it had been any other man he wouldn't have minded?"

"I did not mean that, although perhaps it would have been more understandable. My mother was far from the first woman he had had an affair with."

"I suppose your father told you that, too?"

"It was no secret, believe me."

"If that was the case why was your mother stupid enough to fall for him?" Regan demanded, despising herself for getting into an argument with this young girl, but feeling she had to defend her father at all costs.

Helena went white with anger. "My mother was not stupid, just bowled over by his charm. Your father was a lot older than she, impressing her with his experience, taking advantage of my own papa's preoccupation with his racing, his desire for success."

"My father was a married man—"

"I know that. He treated his own wife abominably. Your mother was filled with such shame over his actions that she took her own life."

Regan paled, dropping down weakly onto the bed. "You—I—what are you saying?"

"It is public knowledge that your mother committed suicide, driven to it by your father's excesses with other women." Helena stared rigidly out of the window.

Regan gave a choked sound of disbelief. "What public knowledge is this? I've certainly never heard of it."

"It was in all the newspapers. Come, you must know it to be true. Why else would you change your name except as a way of not being associated with a man who treated your mother so badly that she had no choice but to take her own life?"

"I didn't change my name," Regan said dazedly. "My aunt and uncle did that when they adopted me."

"Because they did not want to be associated with such a man, either," Helena scorned.

"No! They—"

"They what?" Helena taunted. "Wanted you to be their own little girl? Did they not have children of their own?"

"Two boys," she supplied absently. "Both older than me."

"Then they would not want them tainted by your father's name."

"I don't believe it. My mother was Aunt Edith's sister. They would never have kept a thing like that from me."

"Hah!" Helena scorned. "Most people will do anything to save themselves embarrassment, and you must admit, it would certainly have been that."

"They loved me!" Regan snapped.

"But of course they did. Why else would they have

gone to such trouble to conceal your real identity? But my father was not fooled for one minute."

"They didn't do it to fool anyone. They did it so that I would feel part of their family."

"And now you are part of mine," Helena said with hatred. "The daughter of my mother's lover."

"I won't believe what you're saying!" Regan angrily got to her feet. "It's a lie, something you're making up because you hate me."

"I do not need to resort to lies." The girl sounded curiously like her father. "You do not believe me—I will show you proof."

"Proof?" Regan echoed sharply.

"You do not think I have it?"

"Well, do you?"

"Not personally, but my father does."

"But how—I mean—"

"He is not a stupid man, Regan. When he knew my mother was having an affair with James Matthews he had him investigated. These investigators came up with the story of your mother's misery and death. It was in the newspapers."

"And this proof, where is that?" She felt stunned.

"Downstairs in my father's study. I discovered it in one of the drawers when he sent me in there one day to collect something for him. It is kept locked, of course, but I know where the key is."

"You have a habit of listening to things and looking at things that don't concern you," Regan said bitterly.

"This does concern me!"

"I think it concerns your father and myself, not you."

"Your father killed my mother as well as yours—*that* concerns me. Knowing what sort of man your father was only made him more attractive to my mother, more dangerous, the man every woman wanted to tame. But even my mother couldn't tame him. He was driving like a maniac at the time of the accident."

"Did you get that from the file, too?"

"Yes," Helena said tautly.

"Perhaps these men just told your father what he wanted to hear. After all, it must have been a blow to his pride for his wife to leave him like that." She was clutching at straws now, she knew that, but she didn't want to believe the things this family said about her mother and father.

"Come with me." Helena's fingers bit painfully into her arm. "I will show you everything that is in the file. You will see that it is not possible for so many people to lie about one man."

Regan didn't want to go with her now. If she had any illusions left about her father they were being ripped to shreds by both father and daughter of the Vatis family. But she followed Helena like a lamb to the slaughter.

It didn't feel right to be entering Andreas's study without him knowing about it. But of course if he had known about it they wouldn't be in here. Regan had no doubt that Andreas would not thank his daughter for showing her his private papers.

Helena went straight to the key concealed in a special section of the bookcase, inserting it in the lock to the bottom drawer of the desk.

"I don't think—"

"Scared?" Helena taunted.

"No!" Regan flushed. "But if your father should find out...."

"He would be very angry," Helena confirmed. "But I do not intend telling him, and if you did so you would only be inciting his scorn on you once again. He hates you, does he not?" She took a thick brown folder out of the desk.

"Isn't that obvious?" Regan couldn't help but keep glancing guiltily at the door, expecting Mrs. Hall to come in at any moment and demand to know what they were doing in there.

"Yes," Helena said with satisfaction. She held out the folder. "Here, I hope you enjoy reading it."

Regan watched her walk to the door. "Where are you going?"

"I may not like you," the girl said with studied insolence. "In fact, I dislike you intensely. But if I had to read things like that about my father I would want to be alone...in my shame. Put the folder back in the drawer when you are finished, you know where the key belongs."

Regan stared fixedly at the folder for several long minutes before she could force herself to open the loose cover. After that there was no holding back, each page and photograph more damning to her father's character than the last. The newspaper reports were the worst, the veiled speculation attached to the sudden death of her mother, the insinuations that while her mother had been ill, it had been her lack of a reason for living that had made her die as she did.

With parents like this, what sort of person did that make her!

CHAPTER SIX

THE TRAIN JOURNEY was long and tedious, all the more so because she was desperate to reach London. She had caught the earliest train possible, but even so it was almost evening before she finally left the station. But after tonight she wouldn't be staying in London; she had to go to Scotland and talk with her aunt and uncle.

She had left the house in Cornwall early this morning, long before anyone else was up, and had managed to hitch a lift with a couple driving down for their holiday. They were a nice couple, middle-aged, with a married daughter and young grandchild. Regan had told them her car had broken down, but that she had to get to the station in a hurry. Things had been a bit awkward when the man offered to go back and take a look at the car, but the incident had soon passed over when she told them she had called someone out from a garage.

And now here she was in London, half of her journey over, but still a long way to go. She went straight to the apartment, hoping to beg a bed for the night, too tired to make the rest of her journey today. Luckily Lindy was on her own at the apartment; Chris was on an assignment for his newspaper for a couple of days.

"Job didn't work out?" Lindy asked as she made Regan a cup of tea.

"The job is fine," Regan lied. "I'm just on my way to see my aunt and uncle for a couple of days."

Lindy raised her eyebrows. "Time off already?"

"Well, they were going away and so they said I might as well go home for a while. I haven't seen Aunt Edith and Uncle Fred for such a long time.'' At least that part was true.

"It was nice of Mr. Western to give you the time off.''

"Yes.'' Regan sipped the tea, burning her mouth in her haste. She had forgotten Lindy still thought Clive Western was her employer. And she didn't dare tell her the truth, not when her boyfriend was a reporter. "How is it working out, Chris and you living together?'' She changed the subject.

Lindy shrugged. "Too soon to tell. He's been away since yesterday morning. You are staying tonight, aren't you?'' she said almost pleadingly. "I will go mad if I have to spend another night alone here.''

"Thanks!'' Regan said dryly.

"You know I didn't mean— Hey, that's a nice ring.'' She came over to look more closely at the wide gold band on Regan's left hand. "It looks real,'' she frowned.

Regan snatched her hand away. "It isn't,'' she laughed nervously. "I bought if from one of those little shops down there. It's just junk jewelry.'' It was a Vatis family heirloom, and she should have remembered to take it off before coming here!

"It's lovely. Can I try it on?''

"I— Yes, I—I suppose so.'' She took off the ring, a perfect fit to her finger from the start.

"It's really gorgeous.'' Lindy admired the ring on her own hand before giving it back. "Perhaps you can get me one like it when you go back?''

"Perhaps,'' Regan agreed noncommittally. "Is it okay for me to stay here tonight?''

"Of course. You can have your old room back. Just throw Chris's things on the floor.''

"He is sleeping in there, then?'' she teased.

"Much to his chagrin,'' Lindy laughed. "I don't think he thought I meant it when I said separate bedrooms. He's been so grumpy.''

"Poor boy," Regan laughed, too, finding Lindy's company such a relief after the week she had just spent.

"I think he's getting used to the idea. I'll get dinner while you settle in, then we can sit and watch the film on the box. It will be like old times," she said excitedly.

"I've only been gone a week." But what a week! A disastrous one for her. "You aren't working tonight?"

"Night off. How about spending tomorrow together?"

"I would love to, Lindy, but if I don't leave early in the morning I won't get to my aunt's at all." She had to get away before Andreas realized she was here and came looking for her. He would be getting home sometime today, and as soon as he knew she was missing he would be searching for her. But hopefully not before she had had time to speak to her aunt.

They spent a quiet evening together, Regan half expecting the doorbell to ring at any moment. She shouldn't have come here; she should have gone to a hotel. Andreas would look for her here first.

But no one came to the door that night, and she was able to get away by nine o'clock the next day without anyone but Lindy knowing she had been there.

Two long train journeys in two days made her feel stiff and tired by the time she reached Inverness. Not feeling up to the short walk to her aunt and uncle's house, she telephoned for a taxi to take her there instead. She had missed her aunt and uncle and two cousins, but she knew that it wasn't going to be a pleasant visit, not when she asked Aunt Edith why she had never told her about her mother's death and her father's behavior during, as well as after, the marriage.

She had been to the house in Inverness a couple of times, although not often enough to satisfy her aunt. But it was such a long way to come just for the weekend, making holidays the only real time she could do it in comfort. But she wasn't sure what her aunt would make of her suddenly appearing like this; not that she wouldn't be welcome, but she should have called first.

She paid off the taxi, looking up with relief at the white painted house that partly overlooked the River Ness, the river that flowed out to the beautiful Loch Ness. She and her two cousins, Paul and Donald, had taken a motorboat up the loch last summer. The trip down the loch had been a peaceful experience—the hilly scenery along its banks riveting one's attention—but the trip back!

While they had been out a strong wind had blown up without them realizing it, rocking the boat up and down and terrifying Regan. She had never even been in a boat before, let alone caught up in that sort of wind force. Loch Ness was very long, taking five and a half hours to get from one end to the other—five and a half hours of dipping up and down on what could only be called high waves, making her vow never to go on the loch again.

Regan knocked on the front door. Although sure of her welcome, she couldn't just walk in.

"Regan, love!" Her Aunt Edith smilingly opened the door to her. "Come in."

The two of them hugged each other, Regan handing her aunt the chocolates she had bought for her at the station. If her aunt had a weakness it was chocolates, and her rounded figure confirmed this.

"You shouldn't have," she told Regan, tucking the box under her arm. "Leave your case here," she advised, "and come through to the lounge and have a cup of tea."

Regan put her case down, taking off her jacket. "Are Uncle Fred and the boys here?"

"We're all in the lounge."

"You don't seem surprised to see me," Regan frowned, smoothing her skirt.

"No, well— Come on through." Her aunt seemed slightly flustered, and looking at her more closely she seemed edged with a fevered excitement, a high color to her cheeks. "I've only just made the tea."

"Yes, but—" Her aunt had already opened the lounge door and so she had no choice but to follow her into the room. "Aunt Edith, what—" She broke off, her face paling. Seated beside her uncle on the worn but comfortable sofa was Andreas Vatis! "You!" she choked.

He stood up politely. "Regan," he acknowledged huskily.

"But I— How did you get here?" she asked stupidly, feeling as if all this was happening in a dream, that she was standing outside herself watching this scene, but could do nothing to stop it.

"I came by plane," Andreas informed her, turning to her aunt. "You have already been more than kind, Mrs. Thomas," he spoke smoothly "I hope you do not feel it an impertinence if I ask you if there is somewhere I could talk to Regan alone?" His most charming smile accompanied the request.

"But of course," her aunt fluttered coyly. "You can—"

"Aunt Edith!" Regan said desperately. "Don't you realize who he is? Don't you know that he—"

"I have already introduced myself, Regan," Andreas told her calmly.

"As if an introduction were necessary," Uncle Fred put in lightly.

"But he—"

"That room," Andreas said firmly. "If we could just talk alone?" Once again he smiled at her aunt.

"Take him into the sitting room, Regan," Aunt Edith told her.

"But, Aunt—"

"Come, Regan." Andreas took a firm hold of her arm. "We will not embarrass your family with our discussion."

Her mouth set mutinously as she led him into the room across the hallway from this one. "Why are you here?" She turned on him as soon as the door closed behind them.

He looked down at her haughtily, every inch the arrogant Greek she had come to know...and hate. "I am here to take my wife home."

"I am home," she snapped. "These people are my family."

"*I* am your family," he announced arrogantly. "You are my wife; your place is with me."

"Even if I don't want to be there?"

"Even then," he nodded.

"Let go of my arm," she ordered angrily. "I'm not about to run away. You're the trespasser here."

"Correction, we are both guests of your aunt and uncle. They were only too pleased to allow me to wait for you once I told them we are married."

"How did you know where to find me?"

He shrugged. "They are your only relatives. It is only natural you should come here."

"But why did they let you in? If they know who you are they also know that my father—"

"They know everything, Regan, more than even I realized. But they have never spoken to you about the past, have they?"

"No," she said bitterly. "That was left to your daughter."

"Yes," he agreed grimly. "Something she now regrets...very much."

Regan's eyes widened at the cold anger in his voice. "What have you done to her?"

"I have done nothing to her." He seemed amused by the question.

"I don't believe you. You—"

"You will find there are other ways of punishing Helena other than physically chastising her. She is on Vatis."

"Your island?" Regan gasped.

"Exactly," he nodded. "It *is* an island, somewhere she cannot cause trouble."

"And Tom Stills?"

"Still in Cornwall. So you see, the punishment befits the crime. Helena drove you away from me, and now I have taken her away from the man she is infatuated with."

"You believe me about that now?"

"The scene Helena caused when I told her of my decision to send her to Vatis was more than enough to prove your theory. One day Helena will thank you for being a watchful stepmother."

"I would doubt that!" Regan scoffed.

"But she will. And I thank you now. It was a situation that had not occurred to me." He shook his head.

There was something wrong here. She had expected Andreas to be furiously angry at her sudden disappearance, not thanking her! "Andreas—"

"Yes, Regan?" She had his full attention.

That made her frown even more. During their acquaintance to date it was usually all he could do to acknowledge her existence; to have him actually being nice was reason for suspicion. "Why didn't my aunt and uncle, or at least Paul or Donald, throw you out as soon as they discovered who you were?" Her cousins were both over six feet tall, and surely together more than a match for Andreas Vatis.

"Why should they throw me out?" He raised his eyebrows. "I have done nothing to your family. If you remember, it was all done to me."

"Yes, but—"

"If it makes it easier for you to understand why they did not rush to protect you, I will tell you the explanation I gave them when I arrived. I told them we were married after a whirlwind courtship—"

"It would have to have been," she interrupted dryly.

"When I telephoned them just over a week ago I made no mention of you."

"I realized this, which is why I told them that it was not until after we had been married several days that you discovered the tragic connection between your father and myself, that when you realized what he had done to me you were ashamed, and later fled."

Her eyes were wide with disbelief. "And they believed you?"

"Why should they not?" He looked at her haughtily.

"Because—well, because—"

"Are you not ashamed?" he asked quietly.

"*Yes!* Oh, God, yes." She crumpled down in one of the chairs, her face buried in her hands. "All those reports, the newspaper stories—"

"And that is what most of them were—stories. Innuendos, if you like." Andreas came down on his haunches in front of her, lifting her chin so that she had to look at him. "No matter what those newspapers cared to print, or what Helena enjoyed telling you—" his voice hardened over the last "—your mother did not commit suicide. I admit that she was made unhappy by your father, very unhappy as it happens, but she was not a woman who gave in easily. She was a fighter, like you," he added almost gently.

"Why are you telling me all this?" she sniffed. "I would have thought you, of all people, would have enjoyed seeing my unhappiness. After all, isn't that what this marriage is all about?"

"Calm yourself," he ordered at the shrill rise of her voice. "This marriage is not about making you unhappy. On the contrary, I believe I said I intend to make you very happy."

"In certain areas!"

He nodded distantly. "Perhaps later we will even come to care for each other."

"I doubt it," Regan said bitterly, forcing to the back of her mind the physical effect he had on her.

"We shall see. Now that you have married me the debt your father owed me is paid in full. We must now try to work toward our future together."

Regan jerked away from his caressing hand on her chin. "I don't want a future with you. And I don't see how you can want one with me, not with the sort of parents I had."

His face darkened as he stood up, a frown to his features. "There was nothing wrong with your parents. Your father may have been selfish, egotistical, even a little reckless, but these qualities are not inherent. Your mother was simply a sweet, beautiful woman who married the wrong man for her."

"Why have you suddenly changed your mind about me?" she asked suspiciously. "I thought you wanted me to suffer. And I'm sure Helena thought you would be pleased she had shown me that file."

"I am sure she thought no such thing. She thought only of herself in her plan to get rid of you, of her affection for Tom Stills and her jealousy of you. But she will not repeat the action. She will be a respectful daughter to you."

She shook her head. "I can't see that being true."

"You will see. Now, let us go back and join your relatives, show them that all is well between us before we leave. Come Regan." He put out a hand to assist her to her feet.

She obstinately kept her hand in her lap. "I don't want to leave yet."

"We cannot stay here," he told her firmly.

"*We* can't, but I can."

"You are my wife; your place is at my side. I could still carry out my threat against your father," he added warningly. "You have already seen that I have ample evidence against him."

She took great pleasure in asking him if he really wanted to be involved in such a scandal, although her confidence faded somewhat as he appeared unperturbed.

"It would not bother me," he dismissed. "I would tell everyone how I was tricked, how you used a false name to trap me into marrying you. I can assure you it would be your name that would be blackened, not mine. Do you really want that?"

Her one argument had been stripped from her, leaving her suddenly defenseless. "Why, Andreas? Why do you insist on going on with this?" she pleaded. "I've already suffered more than I can tell you. Isn't that enough?"

"I have just told you that I do not intend you to suffer anymore. Now you must accept being my wife, learn to be the woman at my side, the mother of my children."

"No!" She stood up in her agitation. "No, Andreas, I want to stay here."

He watched her for long, timeless minutes. "Very well," he finally answered. "You may stay—"

"Oh, thank you!" Her eyes shone like sapphires, hardly able to believe his acceptance.

"You did not let me finish," he said firmly. "You may stay until tomorrow—"

"Oh, but—"

"And I will be staying also," he continued calmly.

Regan paled. "You! But you can't! I don't want you here."

"Then we both leave. It is as simple as that, Regan. You are my wife, and if you stay, then so do I. As it happens, your aunt has already invited me to stay the night. I refused at the time, but I can see now that you need this time among people who love you to make the necessary adjustments to accept our marriage."

"I'll never be able to accept that. Never!"

He sighed. "Why do you fight me?" One strong dark hand moved up to caress her pale cheek. "I do not want to hurt you, but if you continue to oppose me I shall have no choice."

Once again Regan was held mesmerized by his touch, the gentle expression in his eyes almost as unnerving. Andreas in this mood she wasn't sure she could handle. "I don't want to fight you, but—"

"Then do not." He pulled her slowly into his arms, cradling her head into his shoulder. "You feel good in my arms, Regan. Do you not think—"

A knock sounded on the door before Aunt Edith came into the room. Her expression softened as she saw Regan in Andreas's arms. "Sorry to interrupt, but I'm just about to prepare dinner, and although you said you wouldn't be staying, Mr. Vatis—"

"Andreas, please," he interrupted smoothly. "And could I possibly change my mind about dinner and also your offer that Regan and I stay the night? Regan has had a couple of tiring days in her flight from me and cannot possibly be made to face another long journey."

"She always was impetuous," Aunt Edith chided. "And we would be pleased if you would stay. You two can have Donald's room—he usually goes in with Paul when Regan comes home."

"Please—" Too late; her aunt had already bustled off to begin preparing the meal. It hadn't even occurred to Regan that she would have to share a room with Andreas. But of course this wasn't Andreas's house in Cornwall with all its bedrooms. This house just had the three bedrooms, and as her aunt and uncle couldn't understand anything but a normal marriage, it wouldn't even occur to them that a couple only married a few days would want separate bedrooms.

"Do not look so worried, Regan." Her husband sounded amused. "This is not the place to make our marriage a reality. When that happens I will want to be completely alone with you, not within earshot of your relatives—especially male cousins of at least six feet who would come running at the least little noise of protest from you.''

"But we'll be sharing a bed!" Bright wings of color heightened her cheeks.

His expression was haughty. "I am not so lacking in control that I cannot spend the night in close proximity to a woman without making love to her."

It was all very well for him to say that, but it didn't stop her dreading the night ahead of them. She was tense all evening, longing for her bed because she was so tired, but fearful of Andreas deciding to come with her. She tried once or twice to get her aunt alone, but each time Andreas would put in an appearance before she had time to say anything of importance to her aunt.

Finally she gave up the struggle to keep awake and announced her intention of going to bed. She looked nervously at Andreas, waiting for his reaction.

"I will join you shortly," he told her quietly, involved in a game of cards with her uncle and two cousins.

"We won't keep him too long." Her uncle's eyes twinkled teasingly.

She made her escape to the sound of the mocking male laughter. It had amazed and surprised her how easily Andreas had seemed to fit in with their simple way of dining and their mild entertainment, used to the more sophisticated way of life as he was. But he had joined in their meal and the family discussion of what program to watch on television that evening as if he did it every day of his life.

Regan had seen another side of him tonight, a side that had charmed all her family, and even made her begin to doubt her impression of him being a cold, cruel man.

She had a quick wash before donning her long cotton nightgown and burrowing down under the bedclothes.

Thank goodness the bed was more or less double size.
But even so, she would still be sharing it with *Andreas*.

She closed her eyes as she heard the bedroom door
open, pretending to be asleep as she heard her husband
moving around the room preparing for bed. Oh, God,
this was worse than she had thought it would be. And as
far as she knew he hadn't brought any clothes with him,
expecting to travel straight back to Cornwall after col-
lecting her.

The light was switched off and she felt the bed give on
the other side as Andreas got in next to her. At least
now she could relax her tightly closed eyelids, although
how she was actually supposed to sleep . . . ! The smell of
Andreas's after-shave and the basic male smell of him
reached out to her in the darkness, making it impossible
for her to even think of relaxing.

"You cannot sleep." His voice sounded strangely removed in the half-light of the room.

"I—I must be overtired." Or just plain scared!

"Would you like me to hold you?"

"No! Er, no." She gave a nervous laugh. "I'll be all
right in a moment."

"If I hold you it will help you relax."

"I—I don't think so." The opposite she would have
thought!

"Would you like to give it a try? Your teeth are chattering with cold—let me warm you."

"No, I—I'll be fine," she lied.

"I have very kindly been loaned pajamas by your
cousin Paul." He sounded amused. "If that is what is
bothering you."

"I see. I—do you usually wear pajamas?" What a
stupid question to have asked. Intimate, too!

"No," he confirmed her suspicions. "Come here."
He pulled her gently into the circle of his arms, settling
her head on his shoulder, his arms around her waist.
"Warmer?" he asked huskily.

The tone of his voice vibrated loudly against the ear resting on his shoulder, a shoulder that was bare. He may have borrowed pajamas from Paul, but he was only wearing the trousers. "Much," she replied, although her teeth didn't stop chattering.

"Have I not told you I will not harm you?" He guessed the reason for her nervousness. "Do you doubt my word?"

"No, of course not." Was that really her voice, that breathless weak sound?

Andreas settled more comfortably in the bed, his arms loosely linked around her. "Good night, Regan."

"You really mean that?"

"I am already half asleep."

His even steady breathing several minutes later pointed to him having fallen asleep completely, although when she tried to move away from him his arms tightened around her.

She was still in his arms when she woke up the next morning, opening her eyes to find him looking down at her.

"In future," he told her huskily, "you will sleep on my left side."

"W-why?" her voice quivered, dreading any future nights they would spend together, knowing they wouldn't be spent as innocently as this one had been.

"Because I cannot see you on this side." He sat up, swinging his legs to the floor, naked to the waist but wearing navy blue pajama trousers.

"I'm sorry, I forgot about your eye."

He pulled on the cotton jacket that matched the blue trousers as a knock sounded on the door. "Come in," he invited softly.

Regan's aunt bustled in with a tray containing cups of tea and a plate of biscuits. "I hope I'm not too early for you." She put the tray down on the bedside table next to Andreas.

"Not at all." He gave his most gracious smile. "Regan and I cannot be too late leaving."

"I'll get your breakfast now, then, shall I?"

The thought of food made Regan inwardly groan. "Not for me, thanks, Aunt Edith."

Her aunt frowned. "You ought to eat, dear. You hardly ate any dinner last night, either."

"I am sure that if you prepare her something she will eat it," Andreas said smoothly. "We have a long way to go, Regan. You should not travel on an empty stomach."

"Maybe some toast," she accepted reluctantly.

"Breakfast in fifteen minutes, then." Her aunt beamed at them both before leaving the room.

"She is a nice lady." Andreas stood up, stretching his arms above his head, his muscles tautly flexed.

Regan turned away. "I think so. I—I'm really sorry I forgot about your eye."

He gave a half smile. "I remember Helena wanting me to resort to wearing an eye patch several years ago. I refused on the grounds that it would make me look like a pirate. I am sure you believe that in marrying you I have behaved like one?"

"Not really." She sipped her tea, still not looking at him. "And I'm glad you don't wear an eye patch. I think one is only necessary if the eye is disfigured and yours certainly isn't." She could afford to be generous; he had kept his promise and left her alone last night. "As you've probably gathered, I can't tell which one is the injured one."

"Except for the scar."

"That's hardly noticeable," she dismissed.

"Nevertheless, you will sleep on my left side," he told her firmly. "It may not be noticeable, but it is completely sightless."

"We—we'd better get dressed. When my aunt says fifteen minutes that's exactly what she means."

"You want me to use the bathroom first?"

She couldn't help smiling. "As long as no one else in the family has claimed it first. Poor Andreas, it isn't what you're used to."

"I have enjoyed my stay here," he said haughtily. "Your relatives are nice people."

"Yes," she agreed huskily. "I'm sure Uncle Fred won't mind you using his razor." His dark growth of beard was very noticeable.

He rubbed his chin. "Perhaps it is as well I did not make love to you last night. This stubble could have done your delicate skin some damage."

Her cotton nightdress was perfectly adequate covering and yet suddenly she felt naked. "I think I just heard someone vacate the bathroom," she murmured quietly.

"Poor Regan," he smiled. "I will leave you now."

She took advantage of his absence to hurriedly dress. She was making the bed when he returned. Her cheeks flushed as she saw there was only the indentation of a head on his side of the bed, she having slept cuddled up to him all night. She had expected to have moved away from him during her hours of sleep, sure that she would be restless with the unfamiliarity of sharing a bed with someone, but to her shame she had stayed in Andreas's arms all night.

"I should hurry with your wash," he advised huskily, noting the bright color in her cheeks. "You aunt has just called us down for breakfast."

Andreas was already seated at the dining-room table when she came down the stairs, although he stood up politely on her entrance. Regan obediently ate the scrambled eggs and toast her aunt had prepared her, ever conscious of Andreas as he ate his eggs, bacon, and grilled tomatoes. Personally, she was dreading leaving here, somehow feeling safe with her family. And yet she had to go; she knew now that Andreas would never

release her. And she did owe him something; he and
Helena both. Her father had ruined both their lives with
his selfishness, and maybe if she could help the difficult
Helena, she would also be helping Andreas.

Her whole family came to see them off, and Regan
felt as if she were saying goodbye forever. No doubt all
brides felt this way as they put themselves into their husband's care.

They went by car to the airport, Andreas dealing with
the formalities while she stood patiently at his side.
They finally went out onto the tarmac to a small jet.

Regan's eyes widened. "Yours?" she asked breathlessly.

"Mine," he confirmed. "As are the pilot and other
crew."

She bit her lip. "I see."

The inside was big enough for twelve people to be
seated in extreme comfort, the seats plush, the floor and
sides carpeted. Andreas's and her seats faced each
other. A young man who looked of Greek birth brought
them drinks once they had taken off.

"How long will it take us to reach Cornwall?" Regan
asked her husband.

"Cornwall?" He was completely relaxed in his seat,
waving the boy away as he came to refill their glasses.
"Later, Niko," he dismissed. "We are not going to
Cornwall, Regan," he told her calmly. "Your aunt very
kindly gave me your passport—we are on our way to
Greece, Regan. To Vatis."

CHAPTER SEVEN

"Why didn't you tell me?" she demanded crossly. "Why go behind my back and ask my aunt for my passport?"

"You were very tired. Yesterday was not the time to discuss it."

"Because you knew I would argue about it!" She hadn't forgotten how remote he said the island was.

"I thought we had agreed we were not to argue anymore."

"*You* agreed I wasn't to argue with you. Really, Andreas, you take too much for granted."

"You knew I must go to Vatis," he said distantly. "Helena is there."

"Yes, but—"

"With Dmitri," he continued pointedly.

She gave him a startled look. "The boy she's engaged to?"

"They are not engaged yet, but they will be. I brought him back from Athens with me. I have had to send Clive Western to Vatis with them to act as their chaperon."

"What excuse did you give for my absence?" She could well imagine his anger when he had returned home with his guest to find his wife missing.

His mouth was grim. "I made Helena tell them that something important had happened in your family, that you had to go to your aunt's for a few days. They had no reason to doubt this. . .or to doubt my wanting to be at your side."

But that he hadn't liked having to lie was obvious,

and she could feel his returned displeasure during the rest of their flight. He made polite conversation with her, talked of Vatis, but he was no longer the almost gentle man he had been at her aunt's.

From the small jet they transferred to a helicopter. Regan's stomach lurched as they took off. Andreas chatted easily with the pilot, seeming not to notice as Regan turned green.

And then the island appeared on the horizon. They had flown across other islands, but she knew this to be Vatis—Andreas suddenly seeming charged with anticipation. It was quite a large island, the house not at first visible among the hilly, tree-covered terrain. And then she saw it, an oasis in a desert. . . or could she mean that the other way around? The island was almost covered in trees except for several roads she could see, and yet quite a large area around the house had been cleared, with lawn as smooth as silk going right up to the door.

They flew over the house, a two-storied villa, a guesthouse set to one side of the lawn, then flew on farther to where Regan could see a landing spot and hangar for the helicopter.

She had known she was married to an arrogant man, a man who commanded and received the best, but seeing him in his own country like this, she realized just what an important man he was. For the first time she began to feel in awe of him.

"Is there anything troubling you?" he asked on the short car journey to the house.

"No," she answered more sharply than she had intended. "Nothing."

"The flight has not unsettled you?"

"Maybe a little." But the subservience of the people she met on this island unsettled her more. First the pilot, then the driver, and now the fat bustling Greek woman who appeared to run the household. Andreas introduced her as Sophia, instructing the other woman to speak English to her new mistress.

"Sophia has looked after me since I was a child," Andreas said teasingly. "She is like a mother to me."

Regan flushed, feeling this last statement had been made as a warning, to tell her that she was not to be rude to the Greek woman. As if she would! "I'm pleased to meet you, Sophia," she smiled at the woman, her height no more than five feet at the most, even making Regan feel tall. "Tell me, what's that lovely smell in the air?"

"That will be the orange and lemon, *kyria*." She received a beaming smile for her interest. "There is a grove of them on the island."

"At least it's cooler here." Regan put her hand through the crook of Andreas's arm. "I know you warned me it would be hot," she smiled up at him with effort. "But I didn't realize it would be quite this warm."

"We can go to the beach later if you are not too tired." The warmth of his voice showed his approval of her behavior. "As my daughter has not come to greet us I assume she is already bathing?" he asked Sophia.

"I am here, papa." Helena bounded up to him, a long-legged creature in clothes that were styled too old for her.

Father and daughter hugged each other. "You appear to be more pleased to see me than you were two days ago."

Helena flushed. "It is not fair of you to remind me of that."

Her father turned her firmly to face Regan. "Greet your stepmother...respectfully," he warned.

"You are well...mama?" Helena's eyes challenged.

"Very well," Regan couldn't help smiling. "You're getting tanned already, Helena."

The young girl's look scorned. "I am naturally dark.

But you should see Clive, papa," her voice softened as she spoke to her father. "He is like a lobster."

Andreas frowned. "You persuaded him to go out in the sun?"

"Well, as Dmitri and I wanted to go waterskiing, he had to come out and drive the boat. Besides, he dare not leave us alone together."

"One of these days, Helena!" her father ground out angrily. "You know the sun upsets him. A few minutes he can stand; hours he cannot."

"But you said I was to get to know Dmitri better," she pouted.

Andreas sighed as Clive entered the villa, a Clive who did indeed look like a lobster. There was a young boy of Regan's age with him, equaling Andreas's dark good looks and build but having none of his harshness. Dark curly hair grew overlong, soft velvety brown eyes were set in a youthfully handsome face, and the tanned muscular body was clothed only in a pair of frayed Levi's. This had to be Dmitri Papalos, the boy Andreas intended Helena to marry.

"You should not have let her do this to you," Andreas told Clive, shaking his head in reproach.

Clive shrugged. "They wanted to ski. Now that you're here could I possibly go back to Athens?"

Andreas smiled and then laughed outright, slapping the other man on the back. He laughed even more as Clive winced. "You can leave now if you would like to. Vittorio will not have put the helicopter away yet."

"I can really go?"

"Yes," his employer smiled. "Be on your way."

"I hope you'll excuse me, Mrs. Vatis." Clive Western's eyes didn't meet Regan's as he spoke to her. "I like the heat, but can't stay out in the sun, and here on Vatis there's little else to do but sit in the sun."

Regan could understand his awkwardness. He must wonder about this hurried marriage to Andreas.

"Please don't let me delay you," she smiled. "I can see you're anxious to get away."

"You know how to reach me if you need me," Andreas reminded as Clive began taking the stairs two at a time. "Now, Helena." He walked his daughter into the cool elegance of the lounge. "What else have you been doing besides tormenting Clive?"

She shrugged. "Just the usual things—swimming, sunbathing."

"And you, Dmitri—" he turned to the young boy "—are you enjoying yourself?"

Dmitri nodded. "Thank you, Andreas." He turned to Regan. "I congratulate you on your recent marriage, Mrs. Vatis."

Andreas frowned. "I have forgotten my manners. I have not introduced the two of you." He made the necessary introductions, watching closely as Regan and Dmitri shook hands.

Regan had changed on the plane at Andreas's suggestion, but nevertheless the cotton dress was now sticking to her. "Could I possibly go to my room?" she asked her husband.

"I will come with you." He joined her at the archway that led to the lounge, its walls white and cool, the goatskin sofa littered with embroidered cushions, and scatter rugs on the tiled mosaic floor. "We need to shower and change. We will join you both later."

He took Regan's elbow as they went up the stairway together. "It is not your room," he told her softly. "Here you will share with me. There will be no dressing room. Sophia and the other servants would not understand such an arrangement. In Greece a man and his wife do not sleep separately."

This came as no surprise to her; after all, he had warned her. But the bedroom did surprise her, both the decor and the huge four-poster bed. It was a beautiful room—the huge furniture of the same period as the bed, the coverlet and curtains of a brocade design. It was like something out of the seventeenth century.

Regan wandered around it, occasionally touching things, finally turning to face Andreas, her eyes shining her pleasure. "It's beautiful," she breathed.

Andreas seemed watchful. "You really like it?"

"Oh, yes!"

"Sophia will be pleased." He seemed relieved. "I have had the servants working hard this last week to have it finished for you."

"For. . . for me?" She looked stunned.

"A new bride deserves a new bedroom," he announced arrogantly. "A bedroom that is suited to her in every way. I knew this was the setting for you the first time I saw you."

"But. . . but the furniture, the curtains. How—"

"All brought over by boat. It has not been easy, I can assure you."

She could see that. But it was a romantic setting, seen through the eyes of a romantic, through Andreas Vatis's eyes! And yet she would have said he didn't have a romantic feeling in his body. Perhaps it had all been done to impress the servants?

"It really is beautiful," she said huskily.

"I am glad you like it."

Was it her imagination or did he sound slightly disappointed with her reaction? What did he expect, that she would throw her arms around him in gratitude? Perhaps if their relationship had been different she might have, but it wasn't, and she had no intention of giving him the impression she liked being in his arms. Besides, she didn't, did she?

"Would you like to use the shower first," she suggested. "I. . . I think I would like to lie down for a while."

He frowned. "You are feeling unwell?"

She was feeling overwhelmed! Just what sort of man

had she married? Until yesterday he had been as cruel to her as he possibly could be; with her aunt and uncle he had been a charming guest, and now here on Vatis he was different again, seeming to lose his harshness and shed the problems that were constantly vying for his attention in England. Here he was just like any other man craving pleasurable relaxation... as long as he didn't expect her to provide it! She had hoped to play the part of his wife by helping Helena accept Dmitri Papalos as her future husband, but by the bedroom she and Andreas were to share it seemed he had quite another role for her to play.

"I've never flown in a helicopter before." She excused her tiredness.

Andreas grinned at her obvious discomfort. "Your stomach is still heaving, hmm?"

She swallowed. "Yes."

He pulled the curtains, and the room darkened instantly, although the cooling breeze still ventilated the room. "Then rest. Too much sun on top of air sickness could make you really ill." His eyes deepened to the emerald color of the sea. "Would you like me to join you?"

"I— No. Please. I—"

"Ah, here is Christina with some fresh orange juice," he interrupted her fumbling refusal, smiling at the young girl dressed in a plain black skirt and white peasant-style blouse, her voluptuous figure shown to advantage in such clothing.

The young girl, probably no more than her own age, smiled shyly. "It is good to have you home, *kyrie*." She turned huge doelike eyes on Regan, her eyes widening as they took in her auburn hair. "Welcome, *kyria*." She seemed mesmerized by Regan's hair, slowly backing out of the room.

Regan frowned. "Why did she—"

Andreas chuckled. "I am sure she thinks I have married a she-devil," he laughed. "Christina does not see a lot of the outside world, preferring to stay on Vatis. Your hair color is not familiar to her. And she was embarrassed because, by the drawn curtains, she presumed we had other plans than my taking a shower and your getting some rest."

Regan blushed. "That's hardly likely, not when Helena and Dmitri are downstairs."

He looked arrogant. "I would not care who was downstairs if I wanted to make love to you. Luckily for you an air flight does little for my sexual inclinations." He threw off his lightweight jacket, beginning to unbutton his shirt. His face darkened at her expression. "I cannot shower fully dressed," he snapped.

"Of course not." She turned away, as for the second time that day his naked torso was revealed to her. God, how different this place was to her aunt and uncle's house. She busied herself pouring out some of the orange juice into one of the glasses. "Would you like some?" She kept her back toward him, sipping the fresh sharpness of newly squeezed oranges.

"Not right now. You may turn around, Regan," he taunted. "I am perfectly decent."

Decent wasn't the word she would have used to describe the way he looked. If by decent he meant he was adequately covered, he was that... just. He was completely naked except for a dark green towel covering his lower half, resting low down on his hips, the dark hair on his chest passing down over his navel and lower. The tan that darkened his already swarthy skin appeared to cover his whole body, making Regan wonder if he swam and sunbathed in the nude. Not with her, she hoped! She was well aware of what a male body looked like, but she had certainly never seen one in the flesh, so to speak.

He shrugged at her silence. "Nakedness is not something to be ashamed of."

"I'm not ashamed!"

"Then why do you turn away?"

Her eyes flashed. "Because all this is strange to me!"

He took a step toward her, the male smell of him reaching out to her. "Then perhaps it is time I became *familiar* to you," he mocked softly.

Regan nervously licked her lips. "I thought you said the flight did. . .did nothing for you in. . .in that way."

Andreas sighed. "You have no reason to fear me, Regan. Even I am inclined to be indulgent among such beauty as you will find on Vatis." He moved to the door that connected them to their bathroom. "But perhaps I should warn you, here on Vatis there is no one to lend me pajamas." He left the room and Regan could hear the soft spray of the shower.

She pretended to be asleep when he returned to their room, keeping her eyes tightly closed as he moved around the room getting dressed. Once he had gone she relaxed, and sleep finally became a reality. Blessed oblivion.

She awoke to the sound of Helena's delighted screams, took several minutes to collect her thoughts together enough to get up from the bed and draw back the curtains to the balcony. Down on the smooth white sand Helena could be seen wrestling with her father, both of them in bathing suits. Helena wore a suit that was again too old for her age—Regan really would have to talk to Andreas about his daughter's clothes—and Andreas wore a pair of navy-blue swimming trunks. He looked like one of the Greek gods, with rip-cord strength in his lean body, the last of conventions finally stripped from him, giving him the look of a pagan.

Regan blushed as he seemed to become aware of her interest and looked up at the balcony. She turned away, hastily going back into the bedroom. She was becoming too aware of Andreas Vatis, seeming sensitive to every movement of his gracefully male body. Oh, God, she couldn't be falling in love with him!

The sleep may have refreshed her, but suddenly she was pale again. Out there on the beach was a man who had every reason to hate her, a man who had married her out of a sense of revenge, who wanted only sons from her, the sons her father had denied him by taking his first wife away from him...and she had made the mistake of falling in love with him! How he would laugh if he knew! His revenge would be complete, his Greek pride appeased.

Regan jumped nervously as a gentle knock sounded on the door. But it couldn't be Andreas; he would hardly knock on his own bedroom door, or so meekly, either. "Come in," she invited.

It was the shy Christina. "The *kyrie* sent me to ask you to join them on the beach," she spoke softly.

So he had seen her! "Thank you," she smiled at the Greek girl. "You speak excellent English, Christina." She made an effort to draw the other girl into conversation, anxious to be accepted here, if only by the staff.

Dark brown eyes lighted up with pleasure. "The *kyrie* taught Vittorio, and Vittorio taught me." She blushed over the last. "Mama helped, too."

Regan remembered that Vittorio was the helicopter pilot, but she had no idea who mama was.

"I am the daughter of Sophia, *kyria*," Christina supplied, "and Vittorio is my husband. In the spring there will be a baby, too," she said coyly. "Shall I tell the *kyrie* you will be down soon?"

"Er, yes. Tell him I'll be there in about ten minutes. And congratulations about the baby." She gave the girl a friendly smile.

Regan took a shower. Lucky Christina, she had it all worked out. She was surrounded by people whom she loved and who loved her, and Regan had no doubt Vittorio was proud of his coming baby. Would Andreas be proud when Regan eventually told him she was having their baby, or would he just accept it as a natural occurrence of their marriage, something that as his wife it was her duty to provide? She had a feeling it would be the latter.

A baby. Andreas's baby. God, what a thought. She looked down at her flat stomach and silky things, imagining herself swollen with Andreas's child. She was still hugging the dream to herself as she wandered back into the bedroom, grabbing her silky wrap as she saw Andreas standing there apparently waiting for her. Her face flamed as she covered her nakedness. So much for imagining carrying his child. She couldn't even let him look at her, let alone have him make love to her!

Green eyes mocked her. "I have left the young ones getting to know each other."

She brushed her hair with nervous jerky movements, unaware that the action pulled the robe tautly across her breasts. "Haven't they been doing that the last two days?" Her recent discovery of her love for him made her shy with him, the happiness of carrying his baby fading as did her girlish dreams of him ever coming to love her. Things like that didn't happen in real life but in storybooks, and this marriage was far from being a fairy tale.

His look was rueful. "I am afraid Clive took his role as chaperon a little too seriously. He has not given them a minute alone together."

"I thought that was the way things happened in Greece."

"Helena is only half Greek. Besides, if Dmitri is to be allowed to sway her affections from Tom Stills then he must be given the same opportunities as him. Tom Stills has been alone with Helena many times." His expression was grim.

"I'm sure he hasn't abused your trust in him, Andreas," Regan assured him, sure that her hair had now been brushed enough but unwilling to turn and face her husband. "So far their mutual attraction hasn't been declared."

"And it will not be!"

"Dmitri seems a nice young man," she said.

"Yes." Andreas eyed her suspiciously.

Regan sighed impatiently. "I meant for Helena, not for me."

"Forgive me," he said surprisingly. "I have no reason to suppose you would be attracted to him."

She was embarrassed by his apology, searching frantically in her mind for something to say to cover the silence that suddenly seemed to surround them. "Christina has just told me she is having a baby." She said the first thing that came into her mind.

Andreas seemed to stiffen, every muscle and sinew tensed as if in anger. And yet he couldn't be angry just because she had mentioned the young girl's pregnancy, could he? "Yes?" he seemed to be waiting, expecting something.

Regan looked puzzled. She shrugged. "Nothing else."

"You do not wish to add anything to your previous statement?" His eyes were narrowed.

"Should I?" she frowned.

"You do not perhaps wish to accuse me of being the baby's father?"

"Certainly not!" Regan gasped. "Why should I think a thing like that?"

He shrugged. "You seem to enjoy thinking the worst of me."

"Perhaps, but I wouldn't accuse you of something like that. Christina seems to be a very nice girl." He began to smile. "What's so funny?" she demanded to know.

"You are. It is not that I am not capable of such a deed; no, it is that Christina is too nice a girl to fall into my lecherous clutches."

"And because she's married to Vittorio!"

"Ah," he nodded. "She told you that, too."

"She seems proud of her young husband," Regan said curtly, still annoyed with him for accusing her of thinking such a thing.

"She has reason to be; he is a good man, a hard worker. Come, get dressed," Andreas ordered briskly. "I think Helena and Dmitri have been alone long enough. I would not like Helena to frighten him off," he added mockingly. "If she does not like someone she does not even attempt to be polite."

"I've noticed." Regan took out her brown bikini.

"She managed to drive you away," he acknowledged. "But you have come back; she will respect you for that."

"I wouldn't count on it."

"I think she will. Hurry," he said impatiently. "Do you not wish to be out in the sunshine?"

"Of course I do, but, well, you— You're in here!" she pointed out desperately.

And he didn't look like moving, either! "I have told you, it is my room, too."

"It may be," she said crossly. "But I'm not some sort of cheap peep show!" She slammed into the bathroom, locking the door after her. She could hear his mocking laughter as he left the room.

Helena and Dmitri were far out to sea windsurfing when Regan got down to the beach. Only Andreas was lazing on the almost white sand, sand that was so hot it seemed to burn the soles of her feet. She put her towel down, wordlessly sitting on it as she rubbed suntan oil on her pale skin. When she had oiled every part of her she could reach she felt the bottle of oil taken out of her hand and raised startled eyes to look into the amused face of her husband.

"Turn around," he ordered. "I will do your back."

"Oh, but—"

"Turn!"

She turned, dreading and yet longing for the sensuous feel of his hands on her body. But he proceeded to rub oil into her skin quite impersonally, although Regan could feel her own tension rising with each stroke of his firm hands against her flesh.

"Do you burn?" he asked huskily.

She wrinkled her nose. "With this coloring, you mean?" She shrugged. "Not usually, although I've never been in sun this strong before."

"Here." He handed her the bottle of oil. "Make sure you keep plenty on, I would hate you to get sunburn." He lifted the hair from her nape, still kneeling behind her as he had been as he oiled her back and legs. Regan felt his lips momentarily caress her neck, stiffening involuntarily at the unexpected gesture. Andreas laughed, slapping her playfully on the bottom. "There is nothing cheap about this body," he mocked her with her own words.

"No, you paid a high price for it," she said bitterly. "Almost too high a price." She inwardly shuddered as she imagined Andreas once again trapped in his racing car, the fear that he must have felt when any moment he might be burned alive. She went paler still as she thought of his beautiful body being hurt any more than it had been. It was like a physical pain to her and she must have recoiled without being aware of it.

Andreas's expression became remote as he moved back to lie on his own towel. "You still hate the thought of marriage to me so much it can make you feel ill," he muttered woodenly.

"Oh, no!" She instantly regretted her impulsive denial as his eyes narrowed. "I...I was just thinking that my father must have been a terrible person to try and injure you in that way."

He raised his eyebrows, dark eyebrows over those startlingly green eyes. "You believe that now?"

Regan sighed. "Yes, I believe it now."

He seemed to hesitate, a dark frown marring his brow. "There is something I think I should tell you, something you must know."

"No, let me finish, Andreas. Please," she added persuasively. "I went to my aunt and uncle's because I. . .I needed to think."

"After what Helena had told you I am not surprised," he said tersely.

"It wasn't really Helena; it was everything, the whole situation. But despite these damning reports you had, I intended to talk to my aunt and uncle about. . .about my mother and father, about the life they had together. But I was coming back to Cornwall when I had found out the truth for myself, when I had had a few days to sort myself out."

"To make me grovel," he reminded her of her threat.

"No." She gave a half smile. "To become the wife you wanted me to be, and to care for Helena."

"And for me also?" he queried huskily.

"No!" She may be prepared to humble herself, but she wasn't prepared to admit to her stupidity in falling in love with him, with a man who could only ever hate her. "No," she repeated more calmly. "But when I got to Inverness everything changed."

"You found me there waiting for you."

"That wasn't the reason it changed," Regan denied impatiently. "It was the love and affection I realized my aunt and uncle must have felt for me, the trouble they had gone to all these years to protect me, to keep the love I had for my father alive. I realized that they must have been suffering all these years, longing to tell me the truth, and yet not wanting to destroy my dreams." There were tears in her eyes now. "I remember once when I was about fifteen I taunted my Uncle Fred for being a stick-in-the-mud, told him that he wasn't fun like my father had been."

"And his reply?" Andreas asked quietly.

"He ruffled my hair and agreed with me. He could say that—" her voice broke emotionally "—when all the time he must have wanted to tell me exactly what sort of man my father had really been. And that's why I didn't ask them about him, didn't let them know that the knight on the white horse had been firmly knocked from his saddle. It would have hurt them, you see, and I...I couldn't hurt them."

"Regan—"

"I haven't finished, Andreas. Please, let me." She couldn't even look at him, knowing that if she didn't say this now then it might never be said. "It was because I didn't want them to suffer anymore that I decided to stop fighting you, why I finally came away with you without protest. So you have your wish, Andreas. I won't fight you anymore."

"Regan, I think you should know—"

"Whew!" Helena threw herself down on the sand next to them. "I'm worn out."

"Helena, Regan and I were talking," her father said sternly.

The young girl flushed, her face embarrassed as she looked at Dmitri. "Would you like us to leave?" she snapped.

Regan could sympathize with her. She was trying to appear adult, and with a few simple words of reprimand her father had reduced her to a child again. Sixteen was an extremely sensitive, delicate age, and Helena felt she had been humiliated in front of the handsome Dmitri.

"That won't be necessary," she smiled at the other girl. "The windsurfing looks fun. Perhaps you could teach me how to do it?"

"Papa is a better teacher than I," Helena told her grudgingly, obviously still disgruntled. "He taught Marisa and I last year."

"Marisa?" Regan echoed sharply. Did Andreas

actually allow his daughter to associate with his mistress?

Helena nodded, beginning to thaw a little. "She came to stay in the guesthouse for a few days while papa was too busy to go to Athens."

Regan stiffened, shooting an angry look at her husband. "And when will she be coming here next?" she asked tautly.

"She will possibly be here during the next day or so," Andreas informed them.

Helena frowned. "But, papa—"

His eyes were cold, his expression remote. "It is my decision," he said tersely.

His decision! To bring his mistress here was *his* decision! Regan couldn't bear it, couldn't bear to see him with the woman who seemed to get most of his time, and possibly even had his heart.

She stood up, her movements agitated. "Excuse me," her voice sounded rather shrill. "I think I'll go in for a swim." She didn't wait to see if there were any objections to her proposal, striking out angrily in the refreshingly cool sea.

Andreas was going to bring his mistress *here*, to keep her right under his wife's nose in the guesthouse. The only thing Regan had to be grateful for was that she hadn't made a complete fool of herself and confessed her love for him.

CHAPTER EIGHT

DINNER WAS A QUIET AFFAIR, eaten quite informally on the terrace that overlooked the sea, although the two men had changed into dark trousers and shirts, and Regan had donned one of the few evening dresses she possessed, and even Helena was wearing more formal attire. But once again the style and color were completely wrong for her youthful beauty; the severe black dress did nothing for her olive complexion, making it difficult for Regan to believe Helena had chosen this herself. She could never be taken for anything but Andreas's daughter even in these awful clothes; her arrogance and breeding were in every gesture she made, but something would have to be done about her wardrobe...and soon.

Regan found a chance to speak to her about it after dinner. The two men were sitting on the terrace smoking cigars and drinking brandy, talking lazily together as she and Helena stood watching the stars. "That's a very elegant dress you're wearing," she said softly to the young girl.

Helena didn't turn. "I hate it," she stated baldly.

Regan's eyebrows rose. "Then why wear it? Why not wear one of your other dresses, one that you do like?"

"I like none of them. They are all like this one," she grimaced. "My Aunt Constantine said it was time I had adult things." She looked down at the gown. "This was what she chose."

So it was an aunt that had the bad taste. Thank goodness it wasn't Helena herself. "It is a lovely gown, Helena—" on a woman of fifty perhaps "—but—"

"Not on me," Helena finished. "I know this. I also know why you are so concerned that I look nice. You want me to marry Dmitri, too, do you not?" she accused. "You want to get rid of me so that you can have papa to yourself." She swung away, walking away from Regan down toward the beach.

Regan saw Andreas move out of the corner of her eye and turned to shake her head as he would have followed his daughter. "I'll go," she told him quietly, pleasantly surprised when he sank back into his chair. "Thank you, Andreas," she said shyly.

He shrugged. "You are her mother now."

Yes, she was, and she wasn't prepared to see the young girl's beauty spoiled by unsuitable clothing when her father could afford to buy her such pretty things. She would have to talk to Andreas about the possible purchase of new gowns later, for now she had to go after Helena.

She caught up with her just as she reached the water's edge. "I don't want to get rid of you, Helena. And you must know that even when you do marry you will always come first with your father." Just as she would always come last!

"That is untrue and you know it," the young girl said bleakly. "Already he puts you before me. I thought he did not love you, that it was because of your father that he married you, but when you went away he came after you. He sent me here."

"I was wrong to let you show me those things," Regan told her gently. "But your father was right to be angry, with us both." And yet he hadn't been with her, he hadn't been!

"It made no difference," Helena shrugged. "You came back."

"And you would rather I hadn't," Regan nodded her understanding.

"Yes. No. I do not know! I am confused. Does my papa truly care for you?"

"What do you think?" Regan evaded a direct answer. She was beginning to think that Andreas might have been right when he said Helena would respect her for coming back, although she wasn't stupid enough not to realize that she had still a long way to go to win Helena's trust. Helping her choose some new clothes would be a start in winning her friendship at least.

Helena shrugged. "I do not know. Sometimes he looks at you and I think he cares very much; other times it is difficult to tell."

By "cares" Regan read "desires." And she knew that Andreas now desired her, that he no longer disliked the idea of making her his wife. She was dreading later tonight when she would have to share that four-poster bed with him, dreading being taken by him when he cared nothing for her.

"I've been thinking about the gowns, Helena," she changed the subject. "How would you like to go to Athens one day and choose some new ones?"

Pleasure blazed in those green eyes so like Andreas's and then was quickly squashed. "It is only a few months since these were bought, and we went to Paris for these."

"You and Aunt Constantine?"

"Papa was in New York at the time. I was staying with his aunt after my illness and she took me to France with her."

"But wouldn't you like new gowns?"

"Not just to impress Dmitri Papalos!" Helena snapped.

"Don't you like him?"

Helena shrugged moodily. "He is all right."

"But not as nice as Tom?" Regan probed gently.

Green eyes flashed with anger. "You told papa about him!" she accused, her young body tensed like a coil.

"*That* is why I am here," she said hotly. "You arranged for papa to send me away from Tom."

"Now, Helena, I—"

"Do not use that reasoning tone with me. I will not marry Dmitri Papalos! I will marry whom I choose! I—"

"You will be silent immediately," interrupted a haughtily chilling voice, "or risk the consequences!"

They both turned to face Andreas, but it was Helena who spoke first. "I will not marry Dmitri, papa," she told him vehemently.

"You seem to be forgetting something, Helena." His voice was soft, dangerously so. "It takes two to make a marriage. Has it ever occurred to you that Dmitri does not want to marry you, either?"

"Not want to marry me?" Helena repeated, stunned.

"That surprises you, hmm?" Her father seemed amused. "But that is the truth of the matter. And I am not surprised at his indecision. You have done nothing to recommend yourself to him. You think of yourself as adult and yet you act like a child, and Dmitri is not sure he wants to marry a spoiled little girl like you. He has gone to his room now because of the scene you are causing."

Helena's eyes were wide with indignation. "He said this to you?"

"Why should he not?" Andreas asked in a bored voice. "You *are* a spoiled little girl."

"I hate you, both of you!" She turned on her heel and ran across the sand to the villa.

Regan gave her husband a reproachful look. "That wasn't kind."

"The truth is often unkind," he said coldly.

"Does Dmitri really not want to marry her?"

"Who knows?" He gave a slight smile. "That was a slight fabrication on my part. But I did not lie when I said she was spoiled."

"But why tell her that about Dmitri?" Regan frowned. "I thought you wanted them to marry?"

"I do, and they will. Helena did not look relieved at his reluctance, did she?" he mused. "She looked outraged."

"Yes," Regan agreed thoughtfully.

"She is angry now, demanding to know in her mind how he dares to reject her. Tomorrow she will set out to capture him, just to show him what he will be missing by not marrying her."

She began to smile, her amusement deepening to laughter as she saw the mischievous twinkle in Andreas's eyes. Andreas in this mood was irresistible. "How well you know a woman's mind."

He shrugged as she still smiled. "At least it has taken her mind off Tom Stills. Come, we will walk together." He put her arm through the crook of his, walking along on the damp sand so that their feet didn't sink in. "He will not be in Cornwall when we return," he told her abruptly.

Regan could only just make out his harsh features as they walked farther and farther away from the lights of the villa. "You dismissed him?"

He seemed to stiffen. "I told you I would not do that. He was contracted for six months; that time will be up while we are here. Next month Helena will return to England to take her examinations."

"Does she know she won't be seeing him when she returns?"

He sighed. "Not yet. But I am hoping that by that time she will not care either way."

"That's hoping for rather a lot," she told him worriedly.

"I am in no hurry to betroth her to Dmitri. As long as she is no longer interested in her tutor I will be happy. How do you like Vatis?" He suddenly changed the subject.

"So far I've found it very enjoyable."

"So far?" The amusement was back in his voice. "You are perhaps expecting that to change later tonight?"

Regan blushed in the darkness. "I told Helena that I would ask you if she could go to Athens to get some new clothes." She deliberately ignored his jibe.

"Did you indeed? And why did you do that?"

"I can't believe that with your own way of always dressing immaculately you haven't noticed how dreadful Helena's clothes are." She was grateful that he didn't pursue the subject of later that night, as she was trying not to think about it.

"I noticed," he agreed. "But she seemed to like them."

"She hates them."

"Then she shall go to Athens as soon as possible. You shall have some new clothes, too."

"What's wrong with the ones I have?" She bristled angrily, considering her own clothes to be attractive if inexpensive.

"Nothing at all. Why is it women always think a man criticizes if he offers to buy them clothes?" He stopped walking, turning in the darkness to look at her, his hands on her upper arms. "I have no complaints about your clothes; on the contrary, the dress you have on this evening is charming—virginal white," he murmured throatily.

It was a pretty dress, just below knee length, white cotton with a square neckline, fitted waist and inch-wide straps across each shoulder. Her skin had tanned slightly golden during this afternoon's laze in the sun, and suited the startling white of her dress.

"But all women like new clothes," he continued huskily.

"You can't buy me with clothes." Regan struggled against the firm hold he had of her.

"I do not intend *buying* you at all! I thought we had agreed I have already paid the price for you. Come, we will not argue, Regan. This is our honeymoon. We have the ideal setting, a beautiful warm night, the stars shining brightly; and the sound of the sea to woo us. Is it not beautiful?"

It was seductive, as he was, and he knew it. "Andreas, please..."

"I do not intend talking anymore. I have better things to do to pass the time."

He was going to kiss her, she knew he was, and yet she didn't move away; her lips even parted invitingly as his dark head bent toward her. Whenever he had kissed her before it had always been as an insult; this time it was different, as his lips parted hers, slowly exploring her mouth as he molded her body against his.

To Regan it seemed as if she were drowning, as if the sea had washed over them both and taken them down into its warm sensual depths, raising them to the heights like a dash of the waves, and then into a calm before raising them again.

Andreas's lips moved from her mouth to her neck, his hands in the glorious thickness of her hair as he explored the sensitive cord in her throat, biting gently on her sensitive skin as her legs began to tremble. "Do I frighten you?" he murmured against her earlobe.

She frightened herself. Her reaction to his passionate kisses made her fearful of her own future, of her independence from this man. He was absorbing her, drawing her into him so that she was mindless, already a part of him. If he were to lay her down on the sand right now and make love to her she wouldn't be able to deny him—she would welcome his possession even, was desperate for release from the emotions he had aroused within her.

"Regan?" He prompted her answer.

"No, Andreas," she said breathlessly. "You don't frighten me."

"You are not cold?" He was still kissing her throat, making her writhe with pleasure.

"No." It was almost a groan.

"I think perhaps you are." His arm remained protectively around her shoulders as he pulled her against his side and began walking back toward the villa. "We will go inside now."

"Yes." She wanted that, wanted more than anything else to be in that four-poster bed with Andreas.

Her arm was around his waist as they entered the villa, nestling against him as he kissed her temple, ruffling the fire of her hair with his lips.

In their bedroom the silk sheet was turned back invitingly, her white diaphanous nightgown laid out across the left side of the bed. Andreas's side was bare, evidence that he had meant what he said about never wearing nightclothes. Regan had a feeling she wouldn't be wearing any tonight, either.

"I'll just go and shower," she said shyly, going toward the bathroom.

"Regan. . ." His husky voice stopped her.

She blushed at the warmth of his gaze. "Yes?"

He picked up the gauzy nightgown. "You forgot this."

Embarrassed, she took it from him. "Thank you."

She hurried with her shower, anxious to be back in her husband's arms, to appear before him in the nightgown he had given her to wear. There was only the light over her side of the bed to illuminate the room when she came back. Andreas was beneath the sheet in the shadow of the right side of the bed. He didn't move as she approached.

He didn't move when she got in the bed beside him and she could see now that he had his back turned toward her. "Andreas," she said softly. No answer.

"Andreas?" Still no answer. He had fallen asleep, the even tenor of his breathing told her.

How could he! How dare he fall asleep after arousing her in that way? He dared because tomorrow or the next day his mistress would be arriving here. Why start a relationship with an unwanted wife when the woman he was really interested in would be arriving soon. Tonight on the beach had just been a mild flirtation on his part, a way of showing her what she was missing, and now he had calmly fallen asleep.

Regan didn't find it so easy; she tossed and turned restlessly, unable to sleep with Andreas lying so close beside her, their bodies occasionally touching. Finally she must have drifted off, although she woke once, only to find herself curved into the back of Andreas's naked body, her arm around his waist. She instantly moved away, huddling onto her own side of the bed.

When she woke in the morning she was alone in the middle of the bed, with no evidence of Andreas's having even slept beside her. Tears welled up and spilled down her cheeks. She was in love with a man who cared nothing for her, who couldn't even bring himself to make love to her.

She was still alone when she went out onto the terrace for breakfast—no sign of any of the others. "Where is everyone?" she asked Sophia when she brought her out a pot of coffee.

"They have gone to Athens, *kyria*." Sophia poured the coffee for her.

"Athens?" she repeated disbelievingly.

"The *kyrie* said he did not wish to disturb you," Sophia eyed her coyly. "He said that you were tired and needed to sleep."

"Yes." Regan blushed. "I—we had a long journey yesterday."

"Of course, *kyria*. What would you like for your breakfast? We have—"

"Nothing for me, thank you, Sophia. I'm not hungry. Did...did my husband say when they would be back?"

"No, *kyria*, but it should not be later than dinner. Will that be all, *kyria*?"

"Yes...thank you." Dinner time! What was she supposed to do here all day on her own? "Er, Sophia?" She stopped the other woman as she was about to leave. "I thought I heard someone riding this morning." She vaguely remembered hearing the sound of horses. "Do we have a stable here?"

The plump housekeeper nodded. "At the back of the villa. And you probably heard the *kyrie*. He always rides early in the morning when he is here."

"Thank you." That solved the problem of what she could do for part of the day.

She spent the morning exploring the island on horseback, riding over the rough terrain with heady pleasure. The young boy in charge of the stables had picked her out a docile mount, a small chestnut mare that handled remarkably well. She discovered the orange and lemon grove Sophia had told her about, and rode through the trees on the hills. She saw several small boats patrolling the shoreline, and recognized them as Andreas's guards. He had told her he had them, and now she had her proof.

After lunch she dozed in the sun, making sure she didn't fall asleep in the heat of the day and get burned. It was after five when she heard the sound of the helicopter returning. She collected up her book and sunglasses and hurried back to the villa, determined to change from her bikini into one of the elegant dresses she had bought in London, anxious not to feel at a disadvantage when she saw Andreas again.

It was obvious the house was inhabited again by the sound of laughing voices and the clatter of feet up the stairs. Regan continued applying her makeup as

Andreas entered their bedroom, her hair already gathered up into a ribbon on the back of her head so that she felt cooler.

"Did you have a nice day?" He shed his jacket, bending down to lightly caress her nape with his lips.

Regan made a definite move away from those probing lips, watching in the mirror as he straightened and stepped back. Her primrose-colored sundress gave her a look of cool beauty, and her voice matched that coolness. "Very nice, thank you," she replied distantly.

"Sophia tells me you have eaten nothing today except a little fruit." He began unbuttoning the cream silk shirt he wore with brown fitted trousers. "Are you still feeling unwell from yesterday?"

"It's so hot I haven't felt like eating," she answered curtly.

He raised dark eyebrows. "The heat is troubling you?"

He was what was troubling her; him and the way her senses were sent spinning just at the sight of him. "A little." She had to give some excuse for her paleness.

Andreas stripped off his shirt completely and threw it onto the bed. "Then it is as well you did not come to Athens with us. Even I found it rather warm there, and I am accustomed to the Greek sun."

"It would have been nice to have been given the option," she snapped.

"You wanted to go to Athens with us?" He sounded surprised by her anger.

Regan swung around on the vanity seat. "Well, that was the idea when I suggested it to Helena."

He frowned. "I took your refusal for new clothes to be a refusal to go to Athens."

Her eyes flashed; she willed herself not to look away as he shed his trousers and pulled on a thin bathrobe. He wasn't embarrassed at her seeing him naked, and she wasn't surprised; she didn't have anyone to compare him with, but she knew his body was magnificent, a truly beautiful specimen of perfect manhood. The sight of him made her tremble, and consequently she spoke much sharper than she intended. "You surely didn't think I would want to be here on my own all day?"

Andreas shrugged. "You have done a lot of traveling the last two days. I thought you would prefer to rest."

Loneliness and a day of brooding were taking their toll. "Why should I need to rest?" Her voice was shrill. "You've done the same amount of traveling and you're a lot older than I am."

His face darkened, his eyes glittering angrily. "You vicious-tongued little—"

A knock sounded on the door. "Regan?" Helena called happily. "Regan, are you in there?"

Andreas grasped her wrist as she would have moved to the door. "Do not answer," he ordered softly. "This conversation is far from over."

"Regan?" Helena sounded doubtful now.

"Stop being so damned selfish," Regan spoke fiercely to her husband. "Don't you realize this is the first time she's ever come to me voluntarily?" She shook off his hand. "And I'm going to answer her whether you like it or not." She swung the door open before he could stop her.

Helena's gaze passed from Regan's defiant face to her father's angry one. "I am sorry," she faltered. "I did not realize you were here, papa. I thought you would be—"

"What do you want, Helena?" he asked tersely. "Can you not see that Regan and I are busy?"

"It's nothing that can't wait." Regan flashed him a look of dislike. "What did you want me for, Helena?" She said, more kindly.

The young girl's shoulders were slumped. "I wanted to show you my new clothes. But it can wait until another time." She shot a nervous glance at her father. "It is not important."

Regan smiled. "I consider it very important. I love looking at new clothes. Come on." She joined the girl outside the bedroom. "You can show me now."

"Regan—"

"We can talk later, Andreas," she told him firmly. Later, when she hadn't been disturbed by his nakedness, when she could perhaps face him on an equal footing.

"Perhaps papa is right." Helena still seemed nervous of her father's unmistakable anger. "You are busy. Later will be all right."

"No, it won't," Regan insisted. "Now let's go before I change my mind." Not that there was much likelihood of that!

"If you are sure. . . ."

"I'm sure." Regan shut the door on Andreas's angry countenance, the reason Helena was still hesitating. "What did you buy?" She walked along the corridor beside the younger girl.

Her eyes lighted up with excitement. "Papa insisted on buying me lots of new things."

Regan laughed. "And I'm sure you told him not to."

"No, I— You are teasing me." Helena gave a rueful smile, taking Regan into her room, where there was box after box of what had to contain new purchases. "Papa has excellent taste," Helena said proudly.

"I'm sure," Regan agreed dryly.

"And he knows exactly the right places to go." Helena began sorting through the boxes.

She was sure of that, too. No doubt he was very generous to his mistresses. She wondered if he had found time to see Marisa during this trip to Athens today. She couldn't see him passing up an opportunity like that. "Did he help you choose all these things?" She was probing for the amount of time he had spent with his daughter.

"Most of them," Helena nodded. "Although he had to call on Marisa for a while."

Oh, God! "Didn't you mind that?"

Helena shrugged. "A daughter has to learn to accept these things."

"A Greek daughter, maybe," Regan acknowledged vehemently. "But not an English wife!" She wouldn't be humiliated like this by Andreas. If he had to carry on with this other woman, it couldn't be for everyone to know, and certainly not his daughter.

"You are angry?" Helena looked puzzled.

"Of course I'm angry! I'm sorry," she said more calmly. "Let's look at your new clothes. Just forget I said anything."

Helena showed her day clothes, evening clothes, clothes for every conceivable occasion—and all of them suitable for a girl of sixteen. Helena was justifiably pleased with her purchases.

"And what was Dmitri doing all this time?"

The sulky look of yesterday came back on Helena's face. "He went to see his family for a while."

"I didn't realize he came from Athens." Although she should have—hadn't Andreas brought him back from a visit to the Greek capital?

"He was bored with the choosing of my clothes. Why did you not come with us, Regan? I thought you were going to."

"Did you want me to?" she asked softly, hopefully.

"Well...I would have liked a female opinion," Helena said grudgingly. "And it was through you that I was able to have the clothes."

"Maybe next time." Regan now knew the reason Andreas hadn't wanted her along—she might have objected to him visiting his mistress.

Helena giggled. "I do not think that will be for some time."

"Probably not." Regan saw four boxes that were still

to be opened and their contents displayed. "You forgot those."

Helena picked up the boxes and put them on the bed. "I did not forget them; they are not mine."

She frowned. "Then whose are they?"

"Yours, of course." Helena smiled. "Papa chose them all himself."

Regan looked at the boxes dazedly. "For me?"

"Yes," the young girl grinned. "Come and see. No, not that one." She removed the top box. "Save that one until last."

The remaining three boxes contained evening gowns—a pure white one, a sophisticated black one, and the last one of sapphire blue, a perfect match for her eyes. They were beautiful gowns and she longed to wear them, and yet they had a stigma attached to them that they had been purchased by Andreas after a pleasant interlude with his mistress.

"Do you not like them?" Helena frowned at her silence.

She gave a bright smile. "They're lovely. I've never owned anything so beautiful."

Helena seemed satisfied with that. "And now for the last box." She placed it expectantly in front of Regan.

She was reluctant to open it, Helena's excitement making her wonder what this final box could contain. When she at last removed the lid she understood Helena's reaction. Inside were lacy bras and matching bikini briefs in half a dozen assorted colors, the garments obviously chosen with pleasure in mind— Andreas's pleasure! Well, he wasn't going to get any from seeing her in the revealing undergarments!

She replaced the lid without a word, putting it on top of the other boxes and picking them all up. "I'll see you later, Helena," she said lightly. "And I like your clothes."

"But not your own, hmm?" Helena said perceptively.

"I like them." But she would never wear them. Never!

Andreas had showered and dressed again by the time she stormed into their room, throwing the boxes angrily down on the bed as he came in from the balcony.

"I see Helena gave you those." He nodded in the direction of the scattered boxes.

"Yes, she gave them to me," Regan bit out. "Now I'll tell you what you can do with them! You can damn well keep them!

He raised his eyebrows. "And what would I do with them?" he sounded amused.

This just seemed to anger her more. "Give them to your mistress! Give them away! I really don't care what you do with them, I only know I don't want them."

"Why?" He sounded calm.

"Because I'm not here to parade in clothing of *that sort*," she shouted at him.

His eyes narrowed. "That sort?" he asked mildly enough.

She threw off the lid to the top box, holding up one of the bras, a pale green scrap of lace that would barely cover her breasts. "That sort," she repeated disgustedly. "If you think I'm going to give you a private show of my body by wearing these, then you're going to be disappointed."

Andreas looked bored by her protestations. "The sight of a female body, clothed or unclothed, holds no surprises for me."

"Oh, I know that. But maybe you get a kick out of revealing underwear like this, maybe—"

"That is enough, Regan!" The quiet authority in his voice cut her off in midflow. "I do not get a *kick* out of revealing underwear. Those things were bought for your pleasure, not mine. You will apologize for that remark immediately."

"Why should I?" she said defiantly.

"Because I have told you ~~you~~ should."

He spoke quietly enough, but she could tell he was furiously angry, coldly, chillingly angry. The fight ebbed out of her. "Maybe I—maybe I misjudged you. Maybe—"

"There is no maybe about it. I am still waiting for my apology, Regan."

One looked at his rigid body and stony face was enough to tell her that neither of them would move out of this room until she had made the apology. But why should she? Okay, so perhaps she had been wrong about the bras and briefs, but he surely couldn't deny he had bought those things as a salve to his conscience after visiting his mistress.

"I don't see why I should," she stubbornly refused. "I know you saw your mistress today, Andreas, and I won't accept these clothes to make you feel better."

"Make me feel better?" he scorned icily. "Giving you gifts does not make me feel anything, you ungrateful little bitch. I do not need such highs when Marisa has already made me feel very good indeed," he added softly, a wealth of satisfaction in his voice.

"Then perhaps you should have stayed with her," Regan snapped.

"And leave my beautiful wife alone for even longer than I did?" he taunted. "Oh, no, Regan, we are man and wife, and I do not intend giving up the pleasure of sharing a bed with you for even one night."

"Is that why you went straight to sleep last night?" She blushed as she realized what she had said. "I meant—"

"I know what you meant, Regan," he said coldly. "I have told you that a Greek wife does not discuss such things."

"And I've told you I'm not a Greek wife!" she said furiously.

"You are *my* wife, and I will make you anything I want to. Now it is time you dressed for dinner. Wear the black gown," he told her arrogantly. "I would wish you to look your best this evening—less the little girl that you undoubtedly are."

"For you?" she sneered.

His mouth tightened. "Not, not for me; for yourself. I am sure that you will want to be your most beautiful tonight."

"Why should I?" she demanded.

"Because you are to meet Marisa at dinner."

Blue eyes opened wide in disbelief. "She's here?" Regan gasped. "On Vatis?"

Andreas nodded. "In the guesthouse, so that she has more privacy. So you see, I did not need to stay in Athens to be with Marisa; I have brought her back here to be with me."

CHAPTER NINE

MARISA LAMOS WAS EVERYTHING Regan had dreaded her
being: beautiful, sophisticated, and worst of all, likable.
She was tall and slender, her hair that silver blond color
occasionally found in Greek women, her face as beautiful as a sculpture.

The two of them met just before dinner. Marisa was
wearing a flaming red gown that seemed to match her
flamboyant, friendly nature. Regan was glad she was
wearing the gown Andreas had suggested she wear, the
black gown a perfect foil for her auburn hair. As much
as she hadn't liked to admit it, Andreas had been right
about her wanting to look her best when she met his
mistress, to show the other girl that he had an attractive
wife, one who intended fighting for him if she got the
chance. If only the other girl weren't so nice!

Andreas had gone downstairs ahead of her, breath-
takingly handsome in a dark green velvet jacket, snowy
white shirt and black trousers. Regan had lingered in the
bedroom, not wanting to look as if she were doing what
Andreas had told her to do, and yet tempted beyond en-
durance to wear the black gown.

It was a straight black sheath of silky material that
outlined each of her curves with intimacy, and, strap-
less, was held up only by the perfection of her breasts.
Her deep auburn hair brushed glowingly around her
shoulders complemented the gown, and after trying it
on she simply couldn't take it off in preference for one
of the gowns she had purchased in London.

She avoided looking at her husband as he introduced

her to Marisa Lamos, unwilling to see the satisfaction in his face. God, how he must be loving this situation!

She gave the other girl a sweet smile. "Andreas has told me so much about you."

Marisa Lamos looked surprised. "That pleases me." She smiled at him as he stood at Regan's side. "But I did not expect him to have spoken to you of his—"

"But of course I spoke of you, Marisa," Andreas cut in smoothly, placing his arm around her slender shoulders. "Are you not invaluable to me?"

Regan turned away from the painful sight of Andreas smiling down tenderly at the other woman. She moved to Helena's side, complimenting her on her new gown, a much more suitable one for her age, its several shades of green suiting her dark coloring.

Marisa sat on Andreas's left during dinner, and he talked in undertones to her all during the meal, leaving Regan to chat to the younger couple. If Helena and Dmitri thought the arrangement odd they didn't show it, and perhaps to them it wasn't. But Regan hated it, hardly knowing how she kept her temper as Andreas smiled and laughed with the other girl.

"How long will she be staying?" she asked tightly as she brushed her hair in preparation for going to bed. The evening had been a disaster as far as she was concerned, having excused herself as soon as she could on the pretense of a headache. She had been more than mildly surprised when Andreas had decided to join her.

He was already in bed, lying back, his arm under his head as a pillow, his eyes lazy as he watched her. Regan was very aware that beneath that silk sheet he was completely naked, his beautiful body as nature had intended it to be. He shrugged now. "She will stay as long as I need her."

Her hairbrush landed with a clatter. "And how long do you think that will be?"

"Perhaps until my wife takes over some of her duties," he drawled.

Angry color rose in her cheeks. "If you mean what I think you mean, you can go to hell!" she blazed at him. "I'm sure Marisa enjoys performing those duties for you; I'd hate to deprive her of that pleasure."

"As you wish." He sounded bored, already turning his back toward her in sleep. "If I am not here when you wake in the morning, I shall be down at the guest-house," he informed her sleepily.

"Wouldn't you rather be there now?"

"Marisa would be as shocked by such an action as you would."

"Oh, I see," Regan scorned. "Everyone in the household knows exactly what's going on, but it mustn't be *seen* to be going on!"

"You are learning fast." He sounded amused.

"I think it's disgusting! In front of your own daughter, too. You—"

"Regan." His soft voice cut across her tirade as he faced her, a warning in his green eyes. "At the moment I could quite easily fall asleep, but if you continue to talk, and consequently to wake me fully, I hope you are prepared to take the consequences."

She blushed at the warmth of his gaze. "I—you—what do you mean?" What a stupid question!

Andreas obviously thought so, too, as he smiled slightly. "I mean it would be a shame to waste this time talking when it could be spent so much more enjoyably...by both of us."

"I wouldn't enjoy being in your arms," she snapped. "Go to sleep, Andreas." She switched off the light before removing her wrap. "Save your strength for your mistress in the morning." Lying beside him under the silk sheet the four-poster bed suddenly didn't seem so huge—it seemed all too small.

Suddenly Andreas had moved and was leaning over

her, her legs pinned to the bed by one of his, his hands holding her arms at her side. "You would dare to issue me orders?" he ground out, dangerously softly.

Sleep was no longer on his mind, she knew that by the hard nakedness of his body as he pressed so intimately against her. "I—I'm sorry, Andreas," she said pleadingly. "I—I'll be quiet now. You...you go to sleep, please."

Her laughter mocked her meekness. "Even a child like you must know that I have decided sleep can wait. It is time my little wife was taught a lesson in pleasing her husband." His lips trailed across her throat, pulling loose with his hands the tie string to the Gypsy-style neckline of her pale blue nightgown. He smoothed the material aside, exposing her already aroused breasts, his mouth teasing and exciting them further to life. "But first I will please you," he murmured huskily. "I shall enjoy that so much more."

Regan knew that she had unwittingly invited this attack, and yet she wasn't altogether sure she regretted it. She liked what Andreas was doing to her, liked his mouth on her body, liked the way his hands caressed her until she trembled with anticipation. In fact, she didn't just like it, she loved it!

Her hands were in the dark thickness of his hair as his lips met hers, exploring and parting her mouth to deepen the kiss to intimacy. His sensual movements were building up a dam of yearned-for satisfaction, a dam that would explode at his possession of her.

"Am I pleasing you?" he asked throatily, his lips against her breast.

"Yes! Oh, yes." Her eyes shone.

He moved away from her as suddenly as he had moved to her side. "I think that is enough in your first efforts to please a man." He watched her with taunting eyes. "Perhaps tomorrow we may continue."

"I—you—" she swallowed hard. "I did nothing to please you!" She lay dazed and *aching* for him.

"It is enough that I pleased you. I like to see you so abandoned." He slowly retied the string to her nightgown. "It would not do for you to know everything at once. Go to sleep now."

"But, Andreas—"

"Sleep." Once again he turned his back on her.

Regan was left with the humiliating feeling that she had once again been an object of amusement to her husband, that he had enjoyed arousing her only to leave her unfulfilled. She also had the feeling that she had just been an hors d'oeuvre to his lovemaking, and that Marisa Lamos would supply the main course.

She was alone when she woke up, hot tears of shame and anger cascading down her cheeks, tears she had suppressed all night long because she couldn't bear Andreas's derision. How was she going to bear this for the rest of her life? Oh, not that she thought their marriage would continue along this sterile vein—she had no doubt Andreas would claim his husbandly rights one day, when he ceased to find her sexual excitement so amusing—but could she bear to live for years knowing that the love she had for him would never be returned. She had thought that by coming here, by becoming his wife, she would save her aunt and uncle any more suffering on her behalf, but she wasn't sure she would be able to bear her own suffering.

Dmitri Papalos was alone on the terrace when she came downstairs, something that surprised her, as Andreas was usually the gracious host. She asked the young boy where Helena was—she already knew Andreas's whereabouts.

He shrugged. "She said she was going for a walk." His English was perfect, as was the English of all the other Greeks she had met.

Regan sat down on the lounger next to his. "Didn't

she ask you to go with her?'' It was the first time she had spoken to Dmitri alone, and she was struck once again by what a really handsome boy he was. Boy! He was only a year younger than she was!

''No,'' he replied moodily.

''Have you been to Vatis before?'' she asked conversationally, doing her best to draw him out. So far he had had a bit of a raw deal as far as this visit was concerned.

''No.''

''Do you like it here?'' she persisted. If she could put up with Andreas's taunting manner she was more than a match for this boy's moodiness.

''We have an island of our own not too far from here,'' he told her in a bored voice.

That didn't surprise her; Andreas would choose a husband for Helena who had as much money as he had. ''Do you want to get married, Dmitri?'' That she had surprised him with the question she could tell by the widening of his velvet brown eyes.

''It is intended that I become betrothed to Helena on her birthday,'' he replied stiffly.

''That didn't exactly answer my question,'' she pointed out gently.

''Of course I wish to marry.''

''I'm not prying, Dmitri. I just want Helena to be happy, for you both to be happy. I don't think either of you is yet ready for marriage. Do you like Helena?''

Dmitri stood up, his back rigid. ''I admire her very much. In time I think I may even come to love her.''

''But not yet?'' Regan probed.

He turned, his face animated for the first time since Regan had met him. ''There is so much I want to do before I marry, so many places I want to see. A wife would stop me doing these things.''

''Have you spoken to my husband, or even Helena herself, about these feelings?''

His expression became resigned. "It would do no good. It has been arranged since childhood that we would marry when Helena is seventeen."

"Well, that's another year away. Couldn't you travel during that time?"

Dmitri shook his head. "My father insists that I enter the family business so that I am able to support my own wife."

So without realizing it Andreas had been right about this young boy's reluctance to marry. Surely he would understand such reluctance—hadn't he expressed regret for being married so young himself? "Have you tried explaining to your father that you want to travel?"

"I tried." He shrugged. "Yesterday I tried. But he would not listen. If I let Helena down I will bring disgrace upon my family. And I would like to marry her. If only it did not have to be now!"

"Would you like me to talk to my husband?" Although whether or not he would listen to her was another matter. "He and your father are friends; I'm sure they could work something out."

Dmitri seemed to doubt this. "I am honor bound to become betrothed to Helena next month and marry her when she is seventeen," he told her haughtily, obviously agreeing with Andreas that a Greek wife should be seen and not heard, and should certainly not try to interfere in such matters as this. "These things are decided by our parents," he added bitterly.

"Yes, but—"

"It is already settled, Mrs. Vatis. If you will excuse me. . . ." He turned on his heel and walked away.

"Enjoying your talk with Dmitri?"

Regan tensed, slowly turning to face her husband. "Very much," she replied. "Did you enjoy your. . . chat with Marisa?" she asked sweetly.

Andreas came to sit on the lounger Dmitri had recently vacated. "What were you discussing so earnestly?" He ignored her question.

"Earnest?" She pretended surprise. "Were we?"

His expression was grim. "It appeared so to me."

"I'm sure you're mistaken." She pushed her sunglasses up higher on her nose. "I was just keeping our guest amused...as you've been keeping Marisa amused."

His mouth quirked. "Not in the same way, I hope."

"And if it were?"

"I would beat you," he told her calmly, "as is my right."

His arrogance made her gasp, especially as he had, to all intents and purposes, just left the arms of his mistress. "And Dmitri?" she asked.

"Would leave immediately. And he would certainly never marry Helena."

"Perhaps I ought to tell him that."

Andreas gave her a sharp look. "What are you saying now? What have you been saying to that boy?"

"I haven't been saying anything. And he isn't a boy; he's nineteen. You were married and almost a father by that time. You knew what you wanted, and so does he."

"I hope it is not you," he said tautly. "I will not let you go as I did Gina."

"Why?" she asked breathlessly, almost hopefully.

"You have not given me my sons yet," he told her arrogantly.

"Oh! Why, you—"

"Calm down, Regan." He was openly laughing at her now. "I am in no hurry."

"Neither am I!"

"Last night I thought otherwise."

Her eyes flashed. "How dare you bring up last night! Just because you can turn your emotions on and off like a tap you think you can taunt me. You found it easy to be like that because you knew you were going to see Marisa today. Where is she, by the way?''

"We went riding early this morning. I would think she is resting."

"Don't you know?'' she snapped.

"Very well,'' he sighed. "She *is* resting."

"I'll bet,'' Regan said resentfully. "I suppose she needs to.''

"I have told you—''

"A Greek wife doesn't discuss such things,'' she finished angrily. "I think Dmitri is of the same opinion.''

"Dmitri?'' Andreas's fingers went around her wrist like a steel clamp. "You have discussed such things with Dmitri?''

How she would have loved to have said yes. But the repercussions for such an action could reach out and touch Dmitri, and while he might be confused about his feelings, she had no doubt that one day he would marry Helena. She couldn't evoke Andreas's anger toward that boy, not even as a means of hitting out at her husband.

"Not those things." She shook off his hand. "I was just asking him how he felt about marrying Helena.''

Andreas's face was grim. "He was right; it is none of your business.''

"I disagree." If anything his face darkened even more. "When you married me you made Helena's happiness my concern.''

"She will be happy with Dmitri.''

"She probably will be...in time. Neither of them wants to marry so young, Andreas." Her voice had softened pleadingly.

His eyes were distant. "He told you this?''

"Yes,'' she answered defensively.

"I have never known such a woman as you!'' he exploded, standing up. "I did not know that you had become so close to Helena and Dmitri that you could tell me what they feel in their hearts," he scorned.

"I haven't," she said impatiently. "But it's obvious—"

"To whom?" he demanded to know. "To whom is it obvious?"

She stood up, too, now facing him defiantly. "To anyone with any sense. Have you ever stopped to ask Helena what she wants, if there is anything *she* would like to do with her life?" All her frustrations of last night were caught up in this vehement argument, all her resentment toward him for mocking her. "No, of course you haven't," she dismissed. "*Asking* isn't your way, is it? You just go right ahead and do what you want to do regardless of anyone else's happiness. Well, I can tell you now that if you force those two to go through with this it will be a disaster. If you left them for a couple of years they would probably marry quite happily. But at the moment they both resent the pressure being put on them."

"Might I remind you that it was your idea that I bring Dmitri and Helena together?" he reminded harshly.

"And I'm glad you did. It's shown me that they both need to live a bit more before even contemplating marriage."

"They have a year."

"A year!" she scorned.

"Am I interrupting?" asked the quietly accented voice of Marisa Lamos. "I can always come back later, but I thought you said you wanted me at ten o'clock, Andreas?"

"I'm just going, Miss Lamos," Regan said haughtily, "so Andreas is all yours." She gave him a defiant look before walking off in the direction of the stables.

She chose the same mare to ride as yesterday, galloping wildly across the island as if the devil himself were at her heels. So Andreas had "wanted" his mistress again at ten o'clock, had he? God, she couldn't take much more of this.

She could see a lone figure on the north beach, long dark hair blowing loose in the wind, the slender shoulders hunched over. Helena! Regan reined in near the other girl. "Is there anything wrong?" she asked gently.

Helena didn't look pleased with this interruption to her solitude. "Nothing. Nothing at all."

"Are you thinking of Tom Stills?"

The startled look on Helena's face showed that he had been the last thing on her mind. In fact, Regan doubted he had been on her mind at all since their arrival here. "Helena?" she prompted.

The girl sank down dejectedly on the sand, and Regan slid off her horse to join her. "Helena, talk to me."

"You will be on papa's side," the girl said moodily, sifting the sand through her fingers.

"There's no pretense between the two of us, Helena, and you know exactly why your father married me. Why should I take his side over anything?"

"Because you got him to bring Dmitri and me here."

"That was when I thought you cared for each other," Regan explained. "But you don't care for him, do you?"

"He is . . . pleasant," Helena said grudgingly.

"But you do not want to marry him," remarked a deep, husky voice.

They both turned guilty faces to look at Andreas. So the devil himself had been after her!

Green eyes flickered over Regan. "Leave us," he ordered firmly.

She glanced apprehensively at Helena. "Do you want me to go?" she asked gently.

Andreas stiffened. "I am perfectly safe to be left alone with my own daughter," he told her coldly.

She blushed. "I know that. I—"

"Then leave us," he repeated curtly.

"Helena?" She stubbornly refused to go.

The girl shrugged. "Papa wishes to talk to me." She accepted the inevitable.

Regan took her time riding back to the villa, unwilling and unable to face Marisa Lamos. If only the other girl wasn't so *nice*. But she was; she treated Regan with respect and friendliness. It didn't seem right that she couldn't even bring herself to dislike the other girl.

As she had thought, Marisa was down on the beach when she returned, and she couldn't just go into the house without speaking to her without seeming rude. She decided to stick to a safe subject. "Have you seen Dmitri?" she asked politely.

Marisa indicated the dark head a couple of hundred yards out from shore as Dmitri swam in the emerald-colored sea. "It is not working out too well between him and Helena." It was a statement, not a question.

Regan's eyes widened. Surely Andreas didn't discuss family business with this woman? She would have thought he could have found a better use for the time he spent with this beautiful woman. "No," she agreed stiffly.

"Andreas is worried, I can tell."

"I'm sure you can," Regan said tightly.

Marisa frowned, her beautiful brow puckered worriedly. "I hope you do not think I am prying, but as Andreas's secretary—"

"Secretary!" Regan repeated astoundedly. "You're his *secretary*?"

Delicate color flooded the normally pale cheeks of the other girl. "I hope you did not think that Andreas and I—"

"No, no, of course not," Regan denied hurriedly. "Andreas just didn't explain the situation very well. I thought perhaps you were a friend of Helena's," she added desperately.

Marisa smiled. "Oh, I am. I have known her all her life. But I am first and foremost Andreas's secretary."

Regan wanted desperately to escape, her embarrassment acute. She looked down ruefully at her sticky shirt and creased jeans. "I hope you'll excuse me while I change?" She smiled, although it was an effort. All she really wanted to do was go to the privacy of her bedroom and give vent to her anger. Andreas had deliberately deceived her about this girl and—

"Regan?" Marisa was giving her a worried glance.

"Sorry," she smiled brightly. "I was miles away. I won't be long; I'll just have a shower and freshen up."

"I will see you later, then."

Regan wasn't too sure of that. By the time she had had this situation out with Andreas he might contrive to keep her in their bedroom. Just let him try!

What she didn't understand was why he had continued to foster her first impression of his relationship with Marisa Lamos. Unless he had taken pleasure from her mistake, had enjoyed her angry accusations as he had enjoyed tormenting her in other ways.

When he strode arrogantly into their bedroom thirty minutes later she was ready for him. She would soon show him that she was no longer fooled by his deception, that she wouldn't be used for his amusement any longer. His first words didn't give her the opening she wanted, but she would wait, oh, yes, she could wait. But not for long!

"I have spoken to Helena," were his abrupt words.

"Well, I realize that," she scorned. "I was there, remember? And being the dutiful daughter that she is you have no doubt persuaded Helena that marriage is the best thing for her."

Glacial green eyes were turned on her as she reclined almost insolently on the bed, her sundress the same blue as her eyes. "This is what you think?" he asked softly.

Regan sat up. "Well, haven't you?"

His mouth was a thin angry line. "I asked if that is what you think has happened."

"But of course." She made no effort to hide her sarcasm, just biding her time until she could tell him she knew of Marisa's true relationship to him. How she would love to see his face when she told him that. "When's the wedding?"

Andreas gave her a narrow-eyed look. "What is the matter with you this time? Are you upset because I wanted to be alone with Helena?"

"Not at all," Regan replied carelessly. "Why should I care about that?"

"You do not care that Helena is not to marry Dmitri?"

Her eyes widened, her own argument with him momentarily forgotten. "She isn't?"

"No. She wishes to go to college and to later perhaps make a career for herself." He shrugged. "She may not like it, but I must give her the chance. It has been arranged that Dmitri will still work for his father, but that he will do all the traveling for the company. Like myself, they have worldwide interests. He will travel as he wanted to do, while still managing to please his father. And he and Helena will be able to meet and fall in love in their own time."

"You've arranged all this?"

"I have been in contact with Dmitri's father on the radio. It seems Dmitri expressed some of his doubts about the marriage yesterday. Paul agrees with me that it would be better to let them wait. You see, we are not ogres."

"Have you told Helena?"

He nodded. "I have told both of them. Already they are liking each other better, behaving more naturally together."

"And Tom Stills?"

"Forgotten," Andreas dismissed arrogantly. "He was not important. I have told Helena of his absence when we return; she did not seem overly worried."

Regan wondered if one day, when he was tired of tormenting her, whether Andreas would dismiss her from
his life as easily as he had poor Tom Stills.

People like them weren't important to people like the
Vatis family, and were easily replaceable.

"Now you," Andreas turned on her coldly. "What is
wrong with you?"

"Me?" She opened wide innocent eyes, standing
up to walk over to the dressing table, the same ex-
tensive array of perfumes here as there had been in
the bedroom at Cornwall. They brought back all too
vividly the way Andreas had contemptuously thrust
one of the bottles at her and asked her to wear it
for his pleasure. She picked up the bottle of Desirable, her fingers curling angrily around its
shape. "There's nothing wrong with me," she told him
tautly. "Whatever gave you the impression that there
was?"

"Perhaps the way you are gripping that bottle, almost
as if it were a weapon."

Until he said these words it didn't even occur to her to
use it as such, but as soon as he had spoken she watched
her arm move almost of its own volition, hurling the
large bottle of perfume through the air like a missile.
Luckily, or unluckily, she wasn't yet sure which, Andreas's reflexes were excellent. No sooner had the bottle
left her hand than he ducked to avoid it.

Regan watched in horror as an angry tide of color
washed Andreas's grim features, his eyes blazingly
angry as he looked disbelievingly from her to the bottle
smashed on the floor behind him. "Why did you do
this?" he asked deceptively quietly, his body tensed like
a coiled spring, seemingly unaware of the pungent smell
of the perfume.

"Because you lied to me." She bravely stood her
ground, wishing with all her heart that she hadn't done
such a stupid thing. What Andreas's retribution would

be she daren't even guess—she just knew it wouldn't be pleasant.

He raised dark eyebrows. "Of what did I lie?"

"Of your so-called mistress." She refused to cower, although God knew she felt like it. She could have hurt him, could have hurt him seriously, and the thought of it made her feel sick. "Marisa told me she's your secretary, so you can stop the pretense now."

He began walking toward her, soft, stealthy steps that reminded her of a jungle cat. "Why should I pretend to you?" he asked contemptuously. "What could I gain from such a deception?"

"Well, I don't know!" she snapped irritably. "But Marisa said—"

"I am sure she did." He was standing in front of her now, his hands moving to painfully grasp her upper arms. "Marisa is hardly likely to tell you the whole of our relationship."

Regan gazed up at him with frightened eyes, no longer able to hide it. "You mean—"

"I mean that she is my secretary, but that it is not the only relationship we have. And now I think it is time our relationship developed along more intimate lines. You have attacked me, accused me, and now it is time to satisfy me. I will delay no longer," he told her harshly.

She gasped at the determination in his suddenly luminous green eyes. "Not now, Andreas! You can't mean to make love to me now," she repeated pleadingly.

"I do not mean to *make love* to you at any time," he dismissed cruelly. "You will become my wife in the fullest sense, but there will be no love attached to the union."

And there wasn't. She fought and clawed at him but in the end it was to no avail, his superior strength holding her captive. Andreas ruthlessly stripped her clothes from her, pinning her arms at her sides as he left not an inch of her body untouched by him. It was as if he were showing her that she belonged to him, that he would touch any part of her he cared to.

There was no tenderness in him as he took possession of her, only the hoarse cry of her name, telling her that he was even aware it was her and not Marisa he claimed.

Regan rolled away from him when it was all over, unable to even look at him. She was too aware that at the last she had been unable to deny the clamoring of her own body for fulfillment, that even though Andreas had merely been using her body she had reached the ultimate in pleasure with him, that they had reached the heights together in shuddering ecstasy. And Andreas had known of the betrayal of her body; he was too experienced a lover not to have known. It was her shame over her reaction to the hard seduction of his body that prevented her being able to look at him, to see the contempt for her there.

She felt him move off the bed, could hear him dressing, and still she couldn't move, couldn't even hide her own nakedness.

"I will send Christina to clean up the mess of the perfume," Andreas said woodenly. "I would advise you to dress before she gets here." The bedroom door closed quietly as he left.

Regan was in the bathroom when Christina arrived, only emerging when she knew she was once again alone. She felt numb; nothing seeming to touch her, everything seeming to happen in slow motion and not making any impression on her.

She refused lunch, staying in her room. She cried off dinner, too, claiming a sick headache. And she did feel sick, sick with herself and Andreas. Not one word had passed his lips as he possessed her—no show of tenderness for the inexperience he had found in her body, and she had to face the fact that Andreas was no nearer loving her than he had been when they first met.

Helena came to her room after dinner, expressing

sympathy for her feeling ill, and respecting her wish to be left alone. The young girl had seemed altogether friendlier, insisting on thanking her for her interference in the wedding plans, even though Regan told her she had nothing to do with Andreas's sudden understanding. If only Helena knew Andreas didn't even enjoy talking to her, let alone actually listening to what she had to say.

Of Andreas she saw nothing. He didn't even share the bedroom that night, and it didn't take two guesses to know where he was or with whom.

The headache she had the next morning was completely genuine, caused mainly through lack of sleep. She couldn't go downstairs and face Andreas; no matter what anyone thought of her she just couldn't leave the sanctuary of the bedroom. As it happened she didn't need to. Andreas himself strode into their bedroom just after nine o'clock.

"Helena tells me you are still feeling unwell." His voice was distant, his dark head held at its usual proud angle. No feelings of remorse here.

Regan cowered beneath the bedclothes, fear in her eyes. "Yes," she confirmed.

"I have come to help you feel better." A bitter smile touched his lips as her fear increased. "Not in that way. I intend leaving Vatis today, in less than an hour in fact."

"L-leaving?" Her eyes widened.

He nodded. "I am going to Athens. I will be taking charge there while Clive goes to England for a few weeks."

"And you're going today?" she asked dazedly.

"Marisa and I will be leaving after we have breakfasted."

A pained dullness entered her eyes. "You're taking Marisa with you."

"But of course. Have I not told you she is invaluable to me?"

"Yes, you told me," Regan acknowledged bitterly. "When will you be coming back?"

His mouth twisted humorlessly. "Do not pretend you would really welcome my return. I am well aware of the fact that after yesterday you cannot even bear to look at me. I will not be returning to Vatis," he said harshly. "In a couple of weeks' time you will return to England with Helena. Eventually I shall join you there."

"Eventually?" she echoed. "When you feel you can tear yourself away from Marisa?"

If anything his expression became even more remote. "I may bring her to England with me. I will let you know at a later date of my plans. But for now I must leave." He turned on his heel and walked to the door.

"Andreas...."

He turned. "Yes?"

"Nothing." She already regretted her involuntary cry of his name. "Have...have a good trip."

"No doubt I shall. Goodbye, Regan."

"Good—goodbye." Her voice broke over the finality of the word. God, please don't let this be goodbye!

CHAPTER TEN

ENGLAND SEEMED VERY COOL after all the Greek sunshine she had enjoyed the last four weeks. Even though it was summer here, too, it could in no way match the heat of Vatis. She and Helena had returned just over a week ago so that Helena could take her examinations.

Regan hadn't so much as spoken to Andreas in that time; all of his radio messages to Vatis and telephone calls to England had been made to his daughter. Helena had not questioned his exclusion of Regan, but was obviously aware of it.

At last she and Helena had become friends, spending most of their time together. They had visited the hairdresser together once back in England, Helena having her long bushy hair shorn to a gleaming bob. It suited her, and threw into prominence her high cheekbones and wide green eyes. It also gave her a more mature appearance, and her attitude seemed to mature with it. She was now looking forward to a further year of schooling, having decided to go back to her boarding school to sit for her A levels, and then she would go on to university if she had the qualifications.

There had been a letter waiting for Regan on her return, and she had eyed it warily for several minutes before deciding this would be the last way Andreas would contact her. The letter turned out to be from Lindy, inviting her to her wedding. The letter made Regan desperate for contact with someone removed from her own unhappiness, and she decided to go to London for a few days and stay at the apartment there.

Helena, as if realizing her need to be alone, didn't press her suggestion that she accompany her.

A couple of days stretched into a week, her reluctance to go back to Cornwall due to the fact that Andreas's personality was firmly stamped all over the house there. As she had realized on her first visit to his apartment—the interview that seemed so long ago—none of Andreas's strength of character had left its mark here. Perhaps that was why she felt she could relax here, briefly forget her marriage to Andreas.

As Lindy's wedding was at the end of the week Regan decided to stay on another week. It hardly seemed worth making the trip back to Cornwall and then coming back again a couple of days later.

She looked up as Margaret came quietly into the room. "Mr. Western is here to see you, madam," she informed her softly.

Regan still found it strange to think of herself as the mistress here, as she was several years younger than the maid. "Please show him in." What on earth could Clive Western want here? Whatever his reason, it was obvious that he was still replacing Andreas at the London office, and Andreas was still in Athens. With Marisa!

She stood up as he entered the lounge, extending her hand in greeting. He seemed to be as nervous as she was.

He sat down at her indication that he should. "I, er, I actually called to see if you're all right."

Regan raised her eyebrows. It felt strange for her to be the one in residence here, and she could sense that Clive felt that, too. "Is there any reason why I shouldn't be?" she asked distantly.

"No, no of course not," he seemed uncomfortable, embarrassed. "I just wondered—"

"*You* did? Or was it Andreas?" she asked suspiciously.

Clive looked startled. "Andreas? Is he here?"

"You're more likely to know his whereabouts than I

am," Regan told him dryly. "I would think I'm the last person he would tell of his movements." She sighed. "If it wasn't he who sent you, then it must have been Helena."

"Yes. She...she called me, asked me if I would look you up and make sure nothing was wrong."

"Considering I only spoke to her on the telephone yesterday evening I'm surprised she should be worried." She had taken to calling Helena every evening, since Helena seemed to want her to.

"Well, she is. I think she has the idea that you've walked out on her, too." Once again he seemed embarrassed.

"Too?" Her eyebrows rose. "I'm sure she realizes her father has work to do, and—"

"I don't mean Andreas." His natural confidence and authority seemed to reassert themselves and his nervousness faded. "I was thinking of Gina."

"Helena's mother?" she frowned. "But that was completely different."

Clive shook his head. "Helena doesn't think so. She's become fond of you, extremely fond I would say, and she thinks you're going to desert her, too."

"But she seemed all right on the telephone last night."

"You should know by now what a tough little character she is. As hard as granite outside, like marshmallow inside. She would never let you guess how vulnerable she really is."

"And yet you've guessed."

"I've worked for Andreas for eight years now; I more or less watched Helena grow up. I'm an honorary uncle, if you like. And right now she's worried and upset, although not for one minute would she let you know that."

Regan came to a decision. "Then she must come here." She had had enough of her own company, and if the truth were known she missed Helena, too. "I'm fond of her, you know."

"Wouldn't it be simpler for you to go back to Cornwall?"

"No!" She instantly regretted her sharpness. "I, er, I can't return yet. I'm going to a wedding in two days' time."

"He's just as likely to come here you know," Clive said gently.

Her body tensed. "Who is?" she snapped.

"Don't play games, Regan. We both know who I'm talking about."

"Andreas," she said dully.

"Of course Andreas." He sighed. "It's none of my business—"

"I agree, it isn't! I...I'm sorry, I didn't mean to snap. But I don't want to talk about him."

His look was compassionate. "Sure?"

"Very sure," Regan assured him tightly. "Now, how would you like to go to a wedding?"

"What?" He looked startled.

Regan laughed. "I don't have a partner for this wedding on Saturday. I wondered if you would take me. Of course, if you have something else to do—"

"I don't," he cut in. "What time is it and where?"

They made the arrangements for him to call for her at the appropriate time and then he took his leave. Regan was looking forward to the wedding, glad that Lindy and Christopher were getting married after all. They had decided that it was a case of sink or swim with regard to marriage and their respective careers, and that it was up to them to make sure they swam. Unfortunately Regan's own marriage seemed to have sunk. She still hadn't told Lindy of her marriage, unwilling as she was to make the explanations that would involve.

She called Helena immediately after Clive had left, assuring her that she would be coming back soon, but in the meantime inviting her up to London to stay with her. Instead of agreeing to this Helena extracted a promise from her that she would return on Sunday, and it was a promise she knew she had to keep. Well, at least one member of the Vatis family seemed to care for her.

God, how she still loved Andreas! She thought of him all the time, dreamed of him all night, and was still no nearer to a solution to this shell of a marriage. She couldn't leave him—he would blacken her father's name and so hurt her uncle and aunt if she did that. And if the truth were known she didn't really want her marriage to end. Unless, of course, Andreas had already ended it; he didn't seem to be making any effort to return to England.

She found herself wondering all the time where he was, if he was still with the beautiful Marisa. It would have been bad enough if he had just been away on business, but the fact that he was in Athens purely and simply to be with his mistress hurt unbearably. Clive Western's holiday would have been over weeks ago, and so there could be no other explanation for this sudden reversal of locations between the two men. She would just have to accept that Andreas would much rather be with Marisa Lamos than with her.

And who could blame him! She hadn't exactly been a complacent wife, and the one time he had made love to her she had contributed nothing to the union. She was sure he didn't get such coldness from Marisa.

How she longed to see him, to beg him to come home if necessary. And yet he wouldn't even talk to her. She had been in the room once when he telephoned, and Helena had asked him if he would like to speak to her. She didn't need to be told his answer. Helena's fiery reaction in Greek had been enough to tell her of his refusal.

SHE WENT OUT ON FRIDAY MORNING and bought herself a new dress for the wedding the next day. Donny Paulos was waiting outside the apartment when she returned.

"How have you been?" he asked huskily.

"Why should you care?" she snapped.

Donny sighed. "He told you."

Regan frowned. "Told me what?"

"Andreas Vatis told you about me. About the way I—"

"Spied on me?" she finished sweetly. "Oh, yes, he told me. Now if you don't mind, I'd like to go inside."

"Regan," he grasped her arm. "Regan, please—"

"Is this man bothering you, Mrs. Vatis?" Albert, the elderly man she had met in reception when she came for her interview, had obviously been watching this encounter and decided she need rescuing.

"It's all right, Albert," she smiled at him. "Donny—Mr. Paulos—is an old friend of mine."

"Well, if you're sure. . . ?"

"I'm sure. Thank you, Albert." The smile left her lips as she looked at Donny. "You had better come in."

She took him up to the apartment, and deposited her shopping in her bedroom before joining him in the lounge.

"So you really are married to him," Donny said dully.

Regan twisted the thick gold wedding ring around and around her finger. "How did you find that out?"

"There was a lot of talk going around the company. You know the sort of thing I mean—like perhaps he will be in a better mood now that he has a beautiful young wife to share his bed. It was not until yesterday that I realized it was you."

"How?" she persisted.

"I was in the office with Clive Western when Helena Vatis's call came in. I understood enough from his side of the conversation to know that you are Vatis's wife."

"Is that any way to talk about your employer?" she taunted.

"I did not know he intended marrying you!" Donny said vehemently.

Regan paced restlessly up and down the room. "And just what did you think he intended doing with me?"

A dark flush colored his cheeks. "I assumed he would—that he would—"

"Oh, I see," she cut in bitterly. "A man like Andreas would hardly sit back and let you escort the woman he wanted!"

"But you are married to him!"

"So I am," she taunted. "But he isn't here with me, is he? His absence should be enough to tell you how our marriage stands. Being a Greek you probably understand this code of revenge your people have."

"Revenge?" His look sharpened. "For what?"

"I don't think that is any of your business," she told him haughtily.

His shoulders slumped. "Probably not. You are unhappy."

"No," she instantly denied, although it had been more a statement than a question.

"You cannot be happy married to a man you do not love and who cares nothing for you."

"You're assuming an awful lot, Donny. What did you get out of this by the way? You were only a clerk the last time we met. What position do you hold in the firm now?"

Again he flushed. "I did not do it for that reason. I—"

"What position, Donny?" she demanded insistently.

His gaze faltered and fell. "I am now the assistant of whoever runs the London office."

"My, my," Regan scorned. "That's some reward for services beyond the call of duty."

"I would not have done it if I had known what he had

in mind. Believe me, Regan, I had no idea he would marry you."

This made her smile, a smile tinged with bitterness. "That only makes it worse. What did you intend doing, Donny? Picking up where we left off once Andreas had finished with me?"

His gaze seemed locked on the shiny tip of his black leather shoes. "Did you not get my telephone messages?"

There had been about half a dozen from him when she had returned from Greece, but she hadn't returned any of them. "Guilty conscience, Donny?"

"Yes!" he snapped. "I wanted to make sure he had not harmed you."

She spread her arms wide. "Well, as you see I'm unharmed and living in the lap of luxury. Now would you mind leaving?"

"Regan—"

"We don't have anything else to say, Donny. And I'm sure your lunch break is up by now. I wouldn't want to blot your record for being a groveling, boot-licking—"

"Enough!" His brown eyes gleamed angrily.

"More than enough," she agreed. "Are you going to leave peacefully or must I have you thrown out?"

His mouth twisted into a sneer. "By that old man downstairs?"

"No." She picked up the telephone and began to dial.

Donny was beginning to look worried now. "You are calling the police?"

Regan shook her head. "Hello?" she said into the receiver. "Mr. Western, please. Mr. Clive Western." She wasn't surprised when a male hand crashed down on the telephone, cutting her off. . .from the Dial-the-Time recording! She had no idea of Clive Western's telephone number. But her ruse seemed to have worked; Donny seemed convinced, anyway.

"There is no need for that," he said angrily. "I will go."

She put the receiver down. "I thought you might."

"I only came to apologize," he told her moodily.

"Apology accepted." She pointedly opened the door, watching him as he walked out. "And, Donny," she said quietly. "I do understand why you did it. My husband is a powerful man. It isn't easy to refuse when he wants something."

His expression lightened. "Thank you," he said almost humbly.

Clive Western didn't seem to know of his assistant's visit to her; at least, he made no mention of it when he accompanied her to Lindy's wedding the next day.

Lindy looked beautiful. The church, the floating white wedding gown, all reminded Regan of what her own wedding had lacked. And Andreas had certainly never looked at her with the adoration Christopher didn't try to hide every time he looked at his bride.

The reception was being held at the apartment, and the forty guests overflowed its four rooms. Clive looked a little overwhelmed, as well he might. Lindy's family was a boisterous lot, but they did make Regan and Clive feel very welcome to their celebration.

"Nice crowd," Clive remarked in the taxi on the way back to Regan's apartment. It was after one in the morning, but even so the party was still going on. Thank goodness Lindy and Christopher had had the good sense to book into a hotel for this one night.

"Very nice," Regan agreed. She had enjoyed herself for the first time in weeks, forgetting her unhappiness for a short time. "Lindy thought you were gorgeous." She smiled as she remembered Lindy telling her to hold onto him.

"She doesn't know you're married, does she?" Clive said quietly.

The smile froze on her lips. "Neither do I half the

time. It's very easy to forget when you haven't seen your husband for weeks.''

"And when Andreas gets back?''

"*If* he gets back." With each passing day she was beginning to doubt that more and more.

"Oh, he'll be back." Clive squashed such thoughts. "And soon."

Regan gave him a sharp look. "You've heard from him about his return?"

"Not exactly. But Athens is my province. I have a fiancée over there. Andreas has always moved around so much it's never mattered where he was based. I like the warmth of Greece; not the sun maybe, but the people, yes, and I like my fiancée most of all."

"Then why holiday in England?" She frowned her puzzlement.

"Holiday? I haven't been on holiday. Andreas radioed me from Vatis and asked me to take over here for a few weeks. This will be the sixth week," he grimaced.

So Andreas had deliberately stayed in Athens from the beginning. She had just assumed Clive was to be on holiday, although thinking back, Andreas had never said he would be. God, how unsatisfactory he must have found her if he had to get away from her the day after making love to her.

"Have you asked him if you can go back?" she asked absently, too stunned to even think straight.

"Repeatedly."

"And he's said no." She sighed. "I'm sorry, Clive. I think I'm the reason England no longer holds any appeal to him."

"I've never understood how you came to be married to him. He told me to give you that job no matter what, but I thought it was a way of helping you, giving you assistance that you were perhaps too proud to accept any other way."

Regan glanced pointedly at the taxi driver. "Shall we discuss this inside?"

She waited while he paid the fare, smiling at the night porter as they went through reception. Jim was a much younger man than Albert, necessarily so if he needed to eject any night callers who weren't wanted.

Margaret had long retired for the evening, but had left the lamps on in the lounge. Regan invited Clive to sit down.

"Coffee?" she inquired.

"No, thanks. You were saying?" he prompted, obviously eager to resume their conversation.

"I wasn't, but I will. The last thing Andreas has ever wanted to be to me is kind." Although there had been a time, at her aunt and uncle's house, when he had been quite gentle with her. But that hadn't lasted long!

"Then why marry you? I'm sorry." He flushed. "I didn't mean that the way it sounded."

"I am sure you did not," drawled a familiar glacial voice.

"Andreas!" Clive and Regan spoke his name together, Clive rising almost guiltily to his feet.

"Good evening...or should I say good *morning*?" Andreas moved out of the doorway that lead to the main bedroom, a menacing figure in black silk shirt and black fitted trousers.

"We've been to a wedding," Regan said defensively. How handsome Andreas still looked to her. She feasted her eyes on him, drinking in every feature, every expression.

"So Margaret informed me," he drawled. "She did not know where, or I might have joined you." He appeared calm enough, but his reference to its being morning proved that he wasn't as cool as he looked.

"It was just at Lindy's," she dismissed. She was glad she was looking her best; the deep green crushed velvet dress made her hair appear more auburn than ever. Oh, *God*, Andreas didn't like her red hair!

"Your ex-apartmentmate?"

She shouldn't be surprised at him knowing that; after all, he had had her watched for ten years. Besides, she remembered it being in that file, the file that had continued about her after her father had died and could no longer be touched. "That's right," she confirmed.

Clive looked uncomfortable. "I think I should be on my way."

"There is no need to leave just because I am here." Andreas sounded as if he were being the pleasant host, and yet Regan knew he was far from being that. His green eyes were like ice, his body rigid with disapproval.

Why was *he* so angry? She had been the one left alone for weeks on end, while he had been in Greece enjoying himself with his girl friend.

"I am sure you would not be leaving so soon if the two of you were alone," he continued coldly. "So please do not leave on my account."

Clive wasn't fooled by his employer's seeming pleasant attitude, either; his quick glance in Regan's direction showed that. "I really do have to go. Thank you for today, Regan. I enjoyed it."

She smiled at him. "So did I."

Andreas's anger seemed to fill the whole room. "Shall I go into another room while the two of you make your goodbyes?" he snapped.

Clive wasn't daunted by the other man's mood; after eight years of working for him he was probably used to Andreas's taciturn nature. "That won't be necessary," he told him calmly. "We've already made them."

"Outside in the taxi, I suppose." Andreas's anger was becoming more and more evident. "Have you been kissing my wife for the whole world to see?" His eyes glittered dangerously.

"I haven't been kissing Regan anywhere," Clive told

him calmly. "I wouldn't even attempt to, but even if I did I'm sure I would get a slapped face for my trouble."

"Would you?" Andreas scorned. "I doubt it."

"Then perhaps you don't know your wife as well as you should. And you can sack me for that if you want to." Clive met Andreas's furious glare unflinchingly. "But I won't stand by and see you malign an innocent girl like Regan."

"Oh, she is not innocent, Clive," he said bitterly. "I made sure of that."

"Andreas!" Regan gasped, her face bright red with embarrassment. "I'm sure Clive doesn't want to hear about our personal affairs."

"Perhaps not," he agreed heavily. "And you still have a job, Clive. You know I cannot do without you. I have booked you a flight back to Greece tomorrow."

Clive instantly brightened. "You're back in England to stay?"

Andreas's glance flickered to Regan. "That depends...on several things. But that will not stop you staying in Athens. I would like to talk to Regan now," he said pointedly.

"Oh...oh, of course, Okay?" he asked Regan softly.

"I am not going to harm her," Andreas rasped harshly.

"I know that. I only—"

"She is my wife, Western! Do not presume on our own friendship to interfere between husband and wife."

"Please go, Clive," Regan pleaded, aware of Andreas's hands clenched into fists at his sides. "I will be all right." She didn't know whether she was relieved or not when he agreed to let her show him out.

"If you need me, Regan, I can be reached—"

"She will not need you." Andreas had followed them and stood watching them angrily. "Now go!" He turned on his heel and walked back into the lounge.

"Please do," Regan encouraged. "And don't worry,

he wouldn't harm me. Have a good flight back to Athens." She smiled bravely as he took his leave, bracing her shoulders as she went back to see her husband.

He was staring grimly out of the window into the darkness, his back rigid. He slowly turned as he heard her return. "How long have you been seeing him?"

"I haven't been 'seeing' him at all. He called Thursday at Helena's request, and so I persuaded him to accompany me to Lindy's wedding."

His mouth twisted. "What form did this persuasion take?"

"Verbal," she informed him tightly.

"And Donny Paulos? What sort of persuasion have you been using on him?"

Regan frowned. "Donny? But I—"

"He came to see me, Regan."

"*Donny* did?"

"Yes," he nodded grimly. "He arrived in Greece this morning, told me exactly what I could do with my job and then walked out."

"The fool." She shook her head. "The stupid, stupid fool. I suppose you intend ruining him now?" she said bitterly, remembering Andreas's original threat to the younger man.

"On the contrary, I intend putting him in charge over here now that Clive has left. I like a man I can respect. By standing up to me as he did Donny Paulos earned that respect."

"And where will you be working if not at the London office?"

He shrugged. "As I told Clive, that depends. I could take over the New York office, or I could run the whole thing from Vatis."

"But I thought you liked the peace and quiet you get there."

"It could still be peaceful and quiet if handled prop-

erly. My business would not be allowed to intrude on...
my other activities.''

Regan licked her lips. "And on what does it depend?''

"On you," he told her bluntly.

"You want a divorce," she acknowledged dully.
"You'll be taking Marisa to Vatis with you."

"Will I?"

"Well, of course, you will. I won't fight you, Andreas.'' She gave a bitter laugh. "What would be the point?''

"Indeed." He nodded arrogantly. "Tell me, Regan, do you think it was rape when I took you?''

Color flooded her cheeks. "No," she admitted huskily.

His eyes glowed like emeralds. "But it was not making love, either, hmm?''

Regan shrugged. "You said it wouldn't be.''

"You hated me for taking your innocence in that way?''

"No!" she denied sharply.

"You acted as if you did.''

"I was ashamed." What was the point in lying now; it was all over.

"Because I aroused you?''

Her eyes flashed as she glared at him. "Can't you leave me with anything?'' she cried. "Not even my self-respect? Of course I was ashamed of reacting to you, you took me with hate—''

"Not hate, Regan," he denied huskily. "Never hate where you are concerned.

She looked at him uncertainly. "But you've always hated me.''

"I have not hated you since you preferred the danger of climbing down a drainpipe to marrying me. I had expected to find a cowed and willing wife; instead I found a virago, a woman who has fought me mentally as well as physically. I began by liking your spirit; I ended up loving you.''

Regan gasped. ''L-loving me?''

His look was haughty. ''You do not believe me?''

''I. . .I don't think I can. The way you've treated me—''

''Has been deplorable. I know this. But I do love you, Regan. I love you very much.'' There was a look of uncertainty about him she had never seen before, a certain vulnerability; his body was tensed as if for a blow. ''My questioning of your actions just now was done because of jealousy of any other men who come near you. I want you all to myself, Regan.''

''But you can't! Marisa—''

''Is my secretary. . .and my cousin.''

''Your. . .your cousin?''

''Yes.''

Her eyes were wide in disbelief. ''And that's the other relationship you have with her?''

''Yes.''

''Nothing else?''

''Nothing,'' he confirmed.

''Then why did you tell me—''

''Because I am a fool!'' A groan came from deep within him. ''You remember I tried to trick Helena into becoming interested in Dmitri by saying he was not interested in her? Well, I tried to do the same to you, only I went a step farther; I let you think there was another woman in my life. It was a stupid thing to do. As was making love to you until you could no longer deny me and then stopping. All that did was put me in agonies all night. You seemed to suffer no effects.''

That's all he knew; she had been in agony, too. She was stunned by these revelations, she couldn't deny she wasn't. And she couldn't believe him. ''Why are you telling me this now?''

He sighed. "In the hope that I can bridge this rift in our marriage."

"A rift you caused," she accused.

"I cannot apologize enough, for the way I took you. I have regretted my actions ever since, but I wanted you so desperately I could hold off no longer. It was—"

"It wasn't that that caused the rift," she told him impatiently. "Going off to Athens with Marisa did that. And spending the previous night with her," she said with remembered bitterness.

"I slept in the room next to you that night. I could hear you moving about, could hear your restlessness, and I knew I had to leave you or risk taking you again. God, Regan, I love you with everything I have, every breath I take!" His hands shook as he ran them through the thick darkness of his hair. "I cannot be near you and not want to take you in my arms and make love to you. I have had to stay away all these weeks because I dared not trust myself not to do more than share your bed."

Regan shook her head. "I don't believe you. You always exercised complete control. You...you even taunted me with my own weakness."

"I have never been in control where you are concerned." He held out his hands. "See, I shake with wanting you."

"I'm still my father's daughter. He still deliberately ran you off the race track and took your wife away from you when you were ill from your injuries."

"The latter he did, but not without Gina's agreement. The former—well, I have a confession to make about that. I have had new evidence about the accident."

"Accident?" she echoed sharply, hopefully. "You called it an accident."

"Because that is what it was. Believe me, Regan, I would not have punished you so if I had not believed my version to be the truth. When your father was killed in that car crash no further inquiries were made on him.''

"No, you passed on to me.''

"If I had not I would have found out that your father was ill, seriously ill. He had a brain tumor.''

"No!'' Regan paled. "He...he couldn't have!''

"He did. He would have blackouts and not know what had taken place during that time. He had such a blackout during the race. I am sorry, Regan, but this is the truth.''

She shrugged off his apology. "Was that why the inquiry was dropped?''

"Yes. As soon as I learned of your father's illness, I looked into the matter of the inquiry. Your father was banned from driving again because of his ill health, although this was never made public knowledge. It was believed he had retired. I thought this myself.''

"When did you find out about his illness?''

"First I have to know if you really want us to divorce. Can you not learn to love me a little, *agapi mou*?'' His voice was huskily pleading. "Forgive me for my harsh treatment of you?''

"How did you find out, Andreas?'' She couldn't give in, not yet, because she had the feeling that once she had confessed her love for him there wouldn't be any words spoken between them for some time, at least none that made any sense.

He drew a ragged breath at the determination in her face. "I had the opportunity to speak with your aunt and uncle before you arrived in Inverness. They inadvertently told me the truth. They believed I already knew of it.''

"Why didn't you tell me the truth then?'' She held her breath as she waited for his answer, so much depending on it.

"Because you would have left me!'' He sounded agonized. "I tried to tell you on Vatis, knowing that you could not get away from me even if you wanted to, but there were always too many interruptions, too many misunderstandings.''

"You loved me even at Inverness?" His sudden change toward her became more understandable.

"Oh, yes." It was a sigh from the heart. "Why do you think I had the bedroom on Vatis especially prepared for you. I had visualized us spending many hours there...together. I wanted you to be happy there, to want to stay there...with me."

"You even love my red hair?" Teasing entered her voice as she felt all barriers between them crumbling.

He picked up one silky strand, letting it run through his fingers. "Especially your red hair. Regan, I love you more than anything else in this world, more even than my own daughter, and if you divorce me I shall be a broken man."

"Not with your strength, Andreas," she denied lightly.

"*You* are my strength. I had hoped—" He broke off with a sigh.

Regan frowned. "Yes?"

He looked down at her with tortured eyes. "I had hoped our union would produce a child, a child that would keep you with me."

"Wouldn't you rather our child was conceived in love?" she asked shyly.

"Mutual love?" he said tautly.

She nodded. "Very mutual. You can take me back to Vatis any time you like, and I'll stay there forever... with you."

"God, Regan." His face was buried in her hair, his arms straining her close to him. "How I have longed for this moment. Tell me, my darling. Tell me you love me."

She took his hand in hers, walking toward their bedroom. "I have a better way of telling you than with words. And you can be sure that this time I won't fight you."

And she did tell him she loved him, time and time again as their love took them to the heavens. Her last thought before she fell into a love-drugged sleep in her lover's arms was that the devil shouldn't be in heaven. But Andreas was her own devil lover, and she would be in heaven with him many times during their lifetime of love together.

For a truly SUPER read, don't miss...

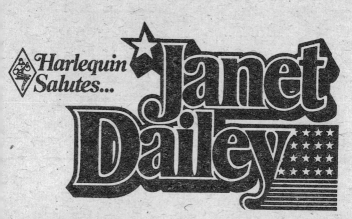

Harlequin Salutes... Janet Dailey

6 best-selling Harlequin Presents titles from the world's No. 1 publisher of romance fiction!

Each tantalizing volume, bound in a distinctive new cover, contains a contemporary love story that will delight you and thrill you—in the true Harlequin Presents tradition!

And now these 6 captivating novels by Janet Dailey are available through Harlequin Reader Service!

Simply complete and mail the coupon on the following page TODAY.

Harlequin Salutes... Janet Dailey

A wonderful opportunity to collect
6 best-selling Harlequin Presents novels by Janet Dailey.

Complete and mail this coupon TODAY.

- -

Harlequin Reader Service

In U.S.A.
MPO Box 707
Niagara Falls, NY 14302

In Canada
649 Ontario Street
Stratford, Ontario N5A 6W2

Please send me the following editions of **Harlequin Salutes Janet Dailey.** I am enclosing my check or money order for $1.50 for each volume ordered, plus 59¢ to cover postage and handling.

☐ **7 Savage Land**
(Presents #139)

☐ **8 Fire and Ice**
(Presents #147)

☐ **9 Valley of the Vapours**
(Presents #183)

☐ **10 Fiesta San Antonio**
(Presents #192)

☐ **11 Show Me**
(Presents #200)

☐ **12 Bluegrass King**
(Presents #203)

Number of novels checked _____ @ $1.50 each =$ _____

N.Y. State and Ariz. residents add appropriate sales tax $ _____

Postage and handling $ __.59

TOTAL $ _____

I enclose _____
(Please send check or money order. We cannot be responsible for cash sent through the mail.)

Prices subject to change without notice.

NAME _____
(Please print)

ADDRESS _____

CITY _____

STATE/PROV. _____ ZIP/POSTAL CODE _____

Offer expires November 30, 1981.

103563124